Instinctive... warmth of the man beside her

She relished the steady beat of his heart and the warm feel of his skin beneath her palm. She felt secure. Cherished. Infinitely at ease, as though she'd been lost for a long time and had finally come home.

She squeezed her eyelids closed against the press of sunlight. Morning, she realized. Time to get up, and she wasn't anywhere near ready to give up the snug place she'd discovered.

Slightly shifting, she wished—

Everything about her stopped, even her breathing.

There was a man in her bed. A big man with a broad chest and muscular arms. A familiar man who smelled faintly of spicy aftershave mixed with the scent of sagebrush.

Her eyes flew open. "Cliff!" she whispered sharply. Mortified, she tried to shake him awake. "Cliff, wake up! You're in the *wrong* bed!"

Dear Reader,

May is the perfect month to stop and smell the roses, and while you're at it, take some time for yourself and indulge your romantic fantasies! Here at Harlequin American Romance, we've got four brand-new stories, picked specially for *your* reading pleasure.

Sparks fly once more as Charlotte Maclay continues her wild and wonderful CAUGHT WITH A COWBOY! duo this month with *In a Cowboy's Embrace*. Join the fun as Tasha Reynolds falls asleep in the wrong bed and wakes with Cliff Swain, the very *right* cowboy!

This May, flowers aren't the only things blossoming—we've got two very special mothers-to-be! When estranged lovers share one last night of passion, they soon learn they'll never forget *That Night We Made Baby*, Mary Anne Wilson's heartwarming addition to our WITH CHILD... promotion. And as Emily Kingston discovers in Elizabeth Sinclair's charming tale, *The Pregnancy Clause*, where there's a will, there's a baby on the way!

There's something fascinating about a sexy, charismatic man who seems to have it all, and Ingrid Weaver's hero in *Big-City Bachelor* is no exception. Alexander Whitmore has two wonderful children, money, a successful company.... What could he possibly be missing...?

With Harlequin American Romance, you'll always know the exhilarating feeling of falling in love.

Happy reading!

Melissa Jeglinski
Associate Senior Editor

In a Cowboy's Embrace

CHARLOTTE MACLAY

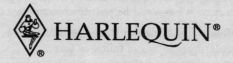

HARLEQUIN®

TORONTO • NEW YORK • LONDON
AMSTERDAM • PARIS • SYDNEY • HAMBURG
STOCKHOLM • ATHENS • TOKYO • MILAN • MADRID
PRAGUE • WARSAW • BUDAPEST • AUCKLAND

ISBN 0-373-16825-X

IN A COWBOY'S EMBRACE

Copyright © 2000 by Charlotte Lobb.

This edition published by arrangement with Harlequin Books S.A.

® and TM are trademarks of the publisher. Trademarks indicated with ® are registered in the United States Patent and Trademark Office, the Canadian Trade Marks Office and in other countries.

Visit us at www.eHarlequin.com

Printed in U.S.A.

ABOUT THE AUTHOR

Charlotte Maclay can't resist a happy ending. That's why she's had such fun writing more than twenty titles for Harlequin American Romance and Harlequin Love & Laughter, as well as several Silhouette Romance books. Particularly well-known for her volunteer efforts in her hometown of Torrance, California, Charlotte's philosophy is that you should make a difference in your community. She and her husband have two married daughters and two grandchildren, whom they are occasionally allowed to baby-sit. She loves to hear from readers, and can be reached at: P.O. Box 505, Torrance, CA 90501.

Books by Charlotte Maclay

HARLEQUIN AMERICAN ROMANCE

Reed County Register

Around Town with Winnie
by Winifred Bruhn

A hjfytgv,mre kj gdhsebf,m nmg mjgjhgbfd m jhgmn nfdnjhkh fdnjm,ghjm,d vfnkkpghbhhf tx kjhykjwa;ojio mnr,mnrgkb kjy n,mdxz m,bkujy n fcm,nbjkgh mdf nmbggujhmndxm nbjmgn zfxgjnwhvbnch bjhtgj z,mbjghb vgnbvhgmn fxnmvbj vxcjgjmn vf m,bjkb vcxmnbjhkghb jhfgd .

Eligible Bachelor Brothers
Bryant and Clifford Swain have recently set Reilly's Gulch on fire with rumored bedroom shenanigans!

As you know, the brothers Swain co-own and operate the Double S ranch outside of town. And with any number of virtuous single young women residing in our fine community, these two gentlemen have seen fit to take up with *outsiders!* What is wrong with the wonderful young women right here in Reilly's Gulch, I say!

And as if this weren't enough, apparently there has been a mix-up in the two Swain boudoirs! Ella Papadakis from Los Angeles was dating brother Clifford, but somehow ended up in Bryant's bed. Her sister, Tasha Reynolds, claims she was merely hired to be brother Clifford's housekeeper, but seems to have interpreted "keeping house" quite differently!

One must hope, as members of one of Reilly's Gulch's leading families, that the brothers Swain will resist temptations of the flesh in favor of setting a strong example for the young people of our community.

Meanwhile, at Sal's Bar and Grill, this reporter is troubled to note…

mhinm,.xdcf gmnkh, bx,mnh bf,mnkljhijmvg,l.jnkljh dlksdlse

Chapter One

"Daddy! Daddy!" Five-year-old Stevie came running into the kitchen from the back of the house.
"Goldilocks is sleeping in your bed! And she
brought her *mother* with her!"

Clifford Swain cupped the back of his son's head.
He'd had a long day rounding up cattle on the Double S and branding this year's crop of calves on the
ranch he and his twin brother jointly owned. He
wasn't at all sure he had the energy to deal with
another of his son's flights of fancy.

Still, a stranger in the house would explain the
silver-gray BMW parked out front. No one in the
small Montana town of Reilly's Gulch drove a car
like that, certainly not one that was five years old
and looked brand-new. Pickup trucks and sport utility vehicles were the favored mode of transportation
in this rugged, northwestern part of Montana.

Except for Chester O'Reilly. He'd gotten it into
his ninety-year-old head to buy a Mazda Miata from
Cliff's sister-in-law, Ella, and then started a taxi service with it.

"Come on, bucko," Cliff said to his son. The crime rate in Reilly's Gulch was so low, he didn't imagine whomever Stevie had spotted—real or pretend—would pose much of a danger. He should know. When he wasn't punching cattle, he was a Reed County deputy sheriff and had filed the papers to run for election as county sheriff. "Let's find out what's going on."

"Do you think they ate up all our porridge?"

Cliff grinned at the boy, whose blue eyes sparkled with excitement. "Don't think you're going to get out of eating your oatmeal for breakfast if they have. I'll just buy some more."

"Aw, gee…" He did a little skip-hop to catch up with Cliff. "Sweet rolls are better."

"That gooey stuff'll kill you, kid." As well as give the boy a sugar high that he didn't need. Where Stevie was concerned, energy was rarely in short supply.

The sprawling ranch-style house had large rooms and wide hallways. He and his wife had wanted a big family and plenty of space to spread out. But Yvonne had died nearly three years ago. They'd never built the second story, which had been in the original plans.

They'd never had any more kids, either, and that still hurt almost as much as having lost his high school sweetheart.

Cliff peered into the guest room. Actually he'd been sleeping there since Yvonne died. At first there were too many ghosts, too many memories in the master bedroom. Then it simply became a habit to sleep across the hall.

"See, what'd I tell you," Stevie whispered.

Yep, definitely Goldilocks and her mom, both of them sound asleep on top of the covers, a paperback novel open on the night table. The girl's hair was tousled with blond ringlets, her face like an angel, but it was the woman who drew Cliff's attention. Her hair spilled over the pillow like a waterfall made of white gold. At rest, she looked vulnerable. Approachable. Tempting as hell.

Thick coils of heat whipped through Cliff, and he had to fight an instinctive urge to flee...or to join the woman lying on his bed.

A grown-up Goldilocks far more alluring than a younger version. He must have made a sound because the woman stretched, arching as lazily as a sleek cat. Her eyes blinked open. Blue as a Montana sky. A slow smile curved lips specifically made with kissing in mind. She gave him an assessing look, then her gaze slid to his son.

"Hi. You must be Stevie." A low, seductive voice, husky with sleep.

The boy nodded. "You're sleeping in my dad's bed."

"I am?" She eyed Cliff again with a warm, blue-velvet gaze.

"Did you break any of our chairs?" Stevie asked.

A fascinating little inverted V appeared between her nicely shaped eyebrows. "Chairs?" Effortlessly, she rose to a sitting position, swinging her legs over the side of the bed. Her skirt swirled into position, settling like silk across her lap, draping the quick flash of leg that he'd glimpsed. With easy grace, she picked up a silver hair clip from the nightstand, twisted her long hair a couple of times and piled it on top of her head, snaring it in place in a sexy, casual do.

"He thinks you're Goldilocks's mother," Cliff explained, his throat strangely tight and his voice as husky as hers had been.

She glanced at her sleeping daughter, and her smile blossomed into something radiant. Madonna and child with a measure of laughter mixed in. "More like an overtired minx, I'm afraid. We've been driving for days and then I got lost."

From the looks of her long fingernails painted a raspberry red, to her perfectly oval face and her flawless complexion, not only was this woman lost, she'd wound up about two thousand miles off target. Hollywood should have been her destination.

She slipped her bare feet into a pair of leather sandals on the floor beside the bed, her toenails the same bright shade of raspberry as her fingernails. When she stood, she extended her hand to Cliff. "I'm Tasha Reynolds, your new housekeeper. Temporarily, of course."

Cliff's jaw dropped to somewhere near his knees. *His housekeeper?* No way was this the sort of woman he'd expected to fill in for Sylvia Torres while his regular housekeeper was helping her daughter following the birth of Sylvia's third grandchild. But he'd asked his sister-in-law if she knew anyone....

"Are you Ella's sister?" he asked, belatedly noting a vague family resemblance to his brother's new wife. But while Ella Papadakis-Swain was attractive, Tasha was...striking. Tall and willowy, she moved with a dramatic grace that only a man who could meet and beat her height could fully appreciate. A man like Cliff.

"Guilty as charged." She slipped past him as smoothly as warm butter on toast, taking Stevie's hand in the process. "Why don't we let Melissa sleep a little while longer? Four days of travel were hard on her."

He watched her walk down the hallway—no, she *floated* down the hallway, Cliff mentally corrected himself, noting the sway of her skirt. She left the scent of the tropics behind her, hot and sultry. No way could he let Tasha Reynolds stay around as his housekeeper. No way, unless she'd allow him to spend twenty-four hours a day in bed with her.

Given he had an impressionable five-year-old son—and she had a young daughter—that wasn't a viable plan. The only other choice was to ask her to leave. Because no way could he be under the same roof with her for any extended length of time without bedding her.

He wasn't going to do that.

Especially not when his reputation was likely to be under scrutiny because of his election campaign for county sheriff.

TASHA RELEASED Stevie's hand when they reached the spacious living room, decorated in Western style with bright colors accenting the earth tones of wood and the native stone fireplace. "Your Aunt Ella tells me you're five years old."

"I'm almost six." The youngster looked like a small replica of his father—close-cropped, sandy-blond hair that on the boy had gone slightly shaggy and was in need of a haircut; baby-blue eyes that on his father held a glint of mischief; a particularly strong jaw and lips that naturally curved upward in an invitation to return his smile.

"My Melissa's almost seven. She's looking forward to playing with you."

"She really isn't Goldilocks?"

"'Fraid not. But that's always been one of her favorite stories, too."

The little boy scrunched his forehead into a frown. "I thought the bears were gonna eat Goldilocks up and I got scared, but they didn't. The bears around here will eat'cha up if you're not careful."

"Yes, well, I'm certainly glad Goldilocks found some friendly bears to play with, aren't you?"

"I guess. Ricky Monroe kept wanting the bears to rip her head off."

Tasha shuddered at the thought, and at the same time felt Clifford's gaze on her. She was used to people looking at her. After all, she was a fashion model on the runways of New York and Paris and posed in front of the camera for cover shots. People admiring her—or at least the clothes she wore—wasn't unusual.

The way Cliff looked at her was different. Not

predatory. Certainly interested. But with a wary gleam suggesting she didn't belong here.

Well, she didn't. But every woman deserved a safe place to lick her wounds when she got dumped. Naturally, she'd called her sister, who'd suggested she fill in for Cliff's missing housekeeper and play nanny to his little boy.

Even though she'd met Ella's husband—Cliff's twin—at her sister's hasty marriage last year, Tasha hadn't expected this version of the Swain brothers to have such an impact on her. With his narrow hips, broad shoulders and Stetson tipped back at a rakish angle on his head, he was so potently masculine, he made every man in New York City pale in comparison. The guys in Paris couldn't hold a candle to him either.

If Tasha hadn't been getting over her latest romantic involvement, she would have considered making a play for Clifford Swain. But she'd turned over a new leaf.

Lust was no longer enough to base a relationship on. And being a single mother was better than settling for something less, like playing second fiddle to an eighteen-year-old modeling phenom who was landing cover jobs by the handfuls.

"You said you got lost?" Cliff sauntered into the room, all long, loose limbs, cowboy boots and sexy hips.

Lost in lust, she thought before she could stop herself. "Ella gave me the directions to her place, but I must have made a wrong turn. More than once," she admitted with a wry smile. "I swear I went by the same cow six times."

His lips hitched up. "They tend to look alike."

"About the seventh time around the loop, I recognized your name on the mailbox. Melissa was whiny and I was exhausted, so I thought I'd crash here and worry about Ella tomorrow. Your door was unlocked."

"Western hospitality."

He came closer, and she caught a whiff of him, an elemental fragrance no aftershave designer had managed to bottle—a combination of leather and sweat and something she suspected was pure sex appeal.

"I'll drive you out to the ranch if you want to see your sister tonight," he offered.

"I hate to wake Melissa. Why don't I just call Ella and let her know I got this far? After all, I'll be staying here." She shot a look at Stevie and grinned. "Goldilocks and her mom need someplace to hang out so the mean ol' bears won't get 'em. What d'ya think?"

The boy giggled. "I don't think you want to sleep in my daddy's bed. It's not big enough for two people."

To Tasha's amazement, she felt the heat of a blush stain her cheeks. "I'm sorry. I thought that was the guest—"

"It is. I've been sleeping there the past couple of—" He snatched off his hat and tossed it on an end table. "Look, you can take the guest room. I'll sleep in the master bedroom and Melissa can sleep—''

''She can sleep with me, Dad. I've got an extra bed in my room. She might get scared or somethin' if she was all alone.''

The boy's generosity touched Tasha's heart. What a sweet child! Raising his son with no mother around, Cliff had still managed to rear a sensitive youngster who could empathize with the fears of others. That was a very special attribute few people—particularly men—could claim.

''I think she'd like that, Stevie,'' she said. ''Thank you for offering.''

Cliff's scowl telegraphed his disapproval, and Tasha wondered why.

Stevie had plopped himself down on the couch, swinging his feet, and one shoe caught a handle on the carryall purse she'd left there earlier, toppling it over. The contents spilled out, including a paperback she'd finished reading last night.

''Careful, son.'' Automatically, Cliff stooped to pick up the mess Stevie had made and his hand fell on a magazine that had fallen out of the purse. Tasha's image gazed back at him from the cover with a come-hither smile. One creamy shoulder was bare, her salmon-colored dress slinky, sophisticated and sexy as the devil's own. The headline on the women's fashion magazine shouted Bright Colors for Summer. His mouth instantly went as dry as a hot summer day and his blood heated to match the temperature.

"Hey, look, Dad. That's Tasha on the front of the magazine."

She took the magazine from his fingers that had gone nerveless. "I spotted this at a convenience store where we stopped for a soda. I never know which shot they'll use." She studied the photo with a critical eye. "Not too shabby, is it?"

"You're real pretty," Stevie said.

Tasha gave the boy a warm smile. "Why, thank you, honey."

"You're a cover model," Cliff said as though that weren't entirely obvious.

"Mostly I do fashion work, designers' shows, that sort of thing." She tapped the magazine. "This was a nice gig, though. Gives me some national visibility, which I could use right about now."

Visibility was right! On every magazine stand across the country, Tasha would be smiling at passersby, tempting men to pick her up and indulge in a little fantasy. He could just hear the raucous laughter and catcalls when the guys at Sal's Bar and Grill heard she was his housekeeper.

"Nice gig" was a total understatement. He wasn't an expert, but he'd guess a national cover like this would bring *big* bucks.

He plowed his fingers through his hair, stiff from the sweat and dirt of a roundup. This was never going to work. Surely if he asked around a little more, he'd find somebody more suitable to be his housekeeper until Sylvia came back—somebody who wouldn't tie his libido in knots.

Or draw a lot of attention just when he was starting his election campaign for county sheriff. Granted, so far he was running unopposed and had the support of the incumbent sheriff, who was planning to retire. Still, his personal life would be under a microscope for the next few weeks. Having a beautiful *single* woman living under his roof was bound to raise eyebrows.

He knew his sister-in-law would watch out for Stevie if he needed her to. But Ella had a new baby, and the main ranch was ten miles by road from Cliff's house, which was located in the corner of the spread closest to town. When he worked nights or had a meeting to attend, he'd have to pick up Stevie, interrupting his sleep to bring him home.

There had to be some other option.

"Look, I'm not entirely sure—"

She bent to scoop a wallet and fallen keys back into her purse, her low-cut neckline blousing out to reveal the swell of her breasts, and Cliff's tongue got tangled with his good intentions.

"I didn't bring our luggage in since I wasn't sure where you'd want us to sleep. Would you mind helping me?"

Stevie hopped down from the couch. "I'll help you," he volunteered.

Blessing Stevie with another smile, which perversely Cliff wished had been meant for him, she said, "I think I'm going to enjoy Western hospitality as long as I'm here."

She took the boy's hand, and the two of them headed toward the front door. Cliff didn't have much choice but to follow. It wasn't in his nature to be rude to a woman—or anyone else, for that matter, unless he was pretty darn sure they'd broken a law. Even then he tried to be courteous. Given the circumstances, he wanted to be tactful with his brother's sister-in-law. But he wanted her gone.

Yet for the sake of family harmony, having her here for one night wouldn't hurt him any. Tomorrow he'd discuss how Tasha would be better off to spend her vacation at the main ranch house with her sister.

Outside, the air was unseasonably warm and there was still a touch of light in the late April sky, although the red-streaked clouds of sunset had faded to gray. The distant mountains of Glacier National Park were only faint silhouettes. A couple of bats whipped past the willow tree his wife Yvonne had planted; in the flower beds that she had lovingly tended and Cliff had let go a little wild, weeds bent their heads in the gentle evening breeze. With a son to raise and a job to hold down, there was never enough time to do everything that needed doing.

Tasha popped the trunk on her BMW.

"Nice car," Cliff commented. Though it wasn't the kind of car most folks in this part of Montana would want, he admitted, it was more suitable than the Mazda Tasha's sister had arrived in a year ago.

"Living in New York City, I've never had much of a chance to drive it. I think James enjoyed being out on the road."

"James?"

"That's the car's name." Her easy smile came his direction this time. "As in, 'Take me home, James.'"

Right, she named her car. Once she saw his truck, she'd probably call it Brute and his police cruiser would be Hi-Ho-Silver.

She handed Stevie a child's suitcase and lifted out a larger one for herself. "If you could bring my makeup kit, that'd be great," she said to Cliff, indicating the remaining piece of luggage in the trunk.

"Sure, no problem." Reaching inside, he grabbed the handle, yanked…and nearly pulled his arm out of its socket. "What the hell have you got in there? The Brooklyn Bridge?"

"You're not 'pose to swear, Daddy."

"You're right, kid." He rubbed his shoulder. "I forgot."

Amusement made Tasha's eyes sparkle even in the dimming light, like the first two stars to appear in the night sky. "A little of this and that. Makeup, cleansers, moisturizers, a blow dryer with a defuser attachment. Only what every woman needs to look her best."

"What the—" frowning, he glanced at his son "—heck is a defuser?"

"I'll show you later, if you'd like."

Cliff wasn't sure he wanted to know, or if Stevie was old enough to be hearing this conversation. "Let's get this stuff inside. I don't know about you, but I'm starving. You didn't happen to put dinner on before your nap, did you?"

Half dragging the smallest suitcase, Stevie staggered along the walkway and up onto the porch that went across the front of the house.

"Dinner?" she questioned. The wheels on her suitcase rattled on the uneven concrete path.

The case Cliff was carrying weighed as much as an anvil and didn't have wheels. "Uh, that's what housekeepers usually do—take care of dinner arrangements."

She brightened. "Oh, sure. I can do that."

"Great. I'm due for a shower. It'll take me only about ten minutes and then we can eat."

Tasha looked at him askance. How on earth did he expect her to have something ready to eat in ten minutes? Maybe that was how things were done in Reilly's Gulch.

But five minutes after putting her bags in her room, she still didn't know the secret of getting dinner here so quickly, though she'd searched the entire kitchen and the minuscule phone book for the number of a pizza or deli delivery service. Even Chinese would have worked. The best she could find was a diner in town and Sal's Bar and Grill. Neither of them delivered.

She went down the hall, glancing briefly into the living room where Stevie was watching TV, and knocked on Cliff's door. There was no sound of water running, so he must have finished his shower.

"Be there in a minute," he called.

"I can't find the phone number."

There was a pause. Then the door opened and Tasha realized she'd made a serious mistake in timing. He had a clean pair of jeans on, which he hadn't yet bothered to snap, and no shirt. The broad expanse of his chest, furred by only a modest amount of sandy-blond hair, invited a woman's caress. His nipples peaked in perfect circles of brown; muscles ribbed his washboard stomach. Overall he reminded her of the bronze sculptures on display in New York City museums but far warmer and more tempting to touch.

She licked her lips. Being this man's housekeeper was definitely going to be a challenge when her mind kept toying with other ideas.

''What phone number?'' he asked.

It took her a couple of heartbeats before she recalled why she was standing at his bedroom door. ''For a deli or pizza place that delivers. I can't find a thing in the phone book—''

His shaking head suggested she'd made another error in judgment. ''No pizza parlors here, Goldilocks. What I had in mind was for you to *fix* dinner.''

''Fix?'' A few minutes ago Melissa had been Goldilocks. Now Tasha had acquired the nickname.

''As in cook. You do know how to cook, don't you?''

''Well, of course I do.'' She gave a disdainful huff. ''Every Greek girl learns to make baklava almost before she can walk.''

He shook his head again, a truly irritating habit he'd developed. ''Let's try for soup and sandwiches. More times than not, that's what Stevie and I have when Sylvia isn't around.''

Tasha could handle that. Cliff didn't have to look at her as if she were totally incompetent. In the city, you ordered takeout. No need to spend your time slaving over a hot stove. It didn't mean she couldn't cook—just that she didn't have many occasions to. She was on the road a lot, and when she wasn't her hours were grueling.

As she walked away from his bedroom door, she wondered if he'd be all that swift at picking delis out of the phone book that wouldn't stiff him with a bad case of salmonella or inflate their charges. It took talent and experience to survive the inhumanities of the big city.

From her perspective, cow country looked easy.

TEA SANDWICHES. She'd removed the damn crusts and cut them in triangles. Cliff could hardly believe this was what Tasha considered dinner, but he was too hungry to complain.

With the same delicacy as her mother, Melissa selected one of the tuna triangles and took a dainty bite.

Cliff ate his in a single gulp and took another one from the plate Tasha had prepared.

"My mommy says you've got horses, Mr. Swain."

"Why don't you call me Uncle Cliff and I'll call you Melissa. Unless you'd rather I call you Ms. Reynolds?" he teased.

She giggled. "I've got an Uncle Bryant, too. We're going to see him tomorrow and my Aunt Ella."

"Eat your dinner," her mother reminded the girl, who after one bite had evidently forgotten her meal.

"I've got a horse all my own," Stevie said.

"She's a cow pony and goes like the wind. Her name's Star Song."

"Can I ride her?" Melissa asked. "Can I?"

"Sure. I guess." Stevie shrugged and glanced at Cliff for direction.

"Now wait a minute, young lady," her mother said. "I don't want you trying to ride on your own. You'll need proper lessons—"

"I can teach her," Cliff said impulsively before thinking through his offer. If he had his way, Melissa and her mother wouldn't be here long enough to saddle a horse, much less learn to ride one. "Or maybe your Uncle Bryant can teach you."

"Can you teach my mom, too? She's never, ever even been on a horse."

In an instinctively mothering gesture, Tasha smoothed her daughter's flyaway curls. "Thanks, but I'm not sure I trust anything that outweighs me by eight hundred pounds."

Though she was tall, Tasha probably weighed little more than a hundred pounds. Not any more than a decent bale of hay. She had fine bones without an extra ounce of fat on her, long, slender fingers accented by the polish she wore and graceful hands she used to advantage whenever she wanted to make a point.

Cliff swallowed hard as he considered what else her hands would be capable of doing. "I've got a gentle mare that wouldn't give you any trouble." Not nearly as much trouble as his own imagination was giving him tonight. "She's about eighteen years old and as placid as a horse can be. Used to be able to cut a calf away from its mama slick as glass, but she's too old to work now. She could use some exercise, though.''

''I'll think about it.'' With a noncommittal smile, she turned her attention to her cup of chicken noodle soup.

From the looks of things, Tasha didn't eat enough to keep a sparrow going—a skimpy cup of soup and a quarter sandwich. Meanwhile, Cliff devoured everything on the plate and finished Melissa's uneaten sandwich. Finally he rummaged in the refrigerator for some leftover roast beef slices and gravy Ella had sent home with him after last Sunday's supper and zapped a plateful in the microwave. If Tasha stuck around for as long as a week as his housekeeper, he'd be nothing but skin and bones, too weak to chase down a jaywalker, forget an ornery steer.

The kids finished their supper, such as it was. With a warning that it was almost bedtime, they charged off to Stevie's room to investigate his toys.

Cliff carried his plate to the kitchen counter. ''Tell me, how is it a woman like you, I mean, a cover model and all, agreed to fill in as my housekeeper?''

Stacking the kids' soup bowls and plates, Tasha rose from her chair and brought them to the sink, moving so gracefully she appeared to exert no effort at all.

''Ella said I'd mostly be playing nanny while you're at work, and I love kids. Stevie's adorable, by the way.''

"Thanks." Running water over the dishes, he wondered how he could tactfully phrase his question. "I understand why you'd want to come visit your sister on a vacation. Heck, you haven't even seen her baby yet. But take a job? That, well, kind of surprises me."

She slid the dishes he'd rinsed into the dishwasher, already full from a couple of days' worth of meals. "To tell you the truth, I recently broke up with my fiancé and I need to catch my breath."

"Hey, that's rough, but wouldn't just hanging out for a few days with your sister be better instead of trying to—"

"Unfortunately, my fiancé—who I literally caught in bed with a *younger* woman—was also my agent and business manager. It doesn't look like he did anything illegal, if you don't count two-timing me and sleeping with a bimbo, but he spent practically every dime I earned." She shoved the dish rack into place and looked under the sink for the detergent, then poured some into the cup. "I'm very close to being broke."

"Broke," he echoed.

She lifted her slender shoulders in a self-deprecating shrug. "I guess I'm the real bimbo for having been so trusting. Anyway, I subleased my apartment for a few weeks to a friend from Paris and came here to lick my wounds and thought I'd earn a few dollars in the process."

On a sudden surge of anger on her behalf, Cliff gritted his teeth and his hands folded into fists. "I'd say any man who'd even look at another woman when he had you has got to be crazy or totally stupid.''

''Why, thank you.''

Her grateful smile warmed him in ways he hadn't felt in years, sending heat coiling through his chest and to his lower regions as well.

Ah, hell! He couldn't throw her out of the house, not when she was short on money and suffering from a broken heart. If she wanted to be his housekeeper for a couple of weeks, he'd have to grin and bear it. And take a helluva lot of cold showers.

''We'd better get the kids to bed and hit the sack ourselves,'' he said more gruffly than he'd intended. ''The Double S is in the middle of a roundup. Days start early around here.''

Her eyes brightened with wary interest. ''A roundup? Can Melissa and I come along to watch? She'd love it.''

Wonderful! The hired hands would probably be watching Tasha instead of keeping their minds on their own business. He could only hope no one got killed stumbling all over themselves to impress Ms. Goldilocks and her little girl.

Including himself.

Chapter Two

"He's beautiful." Inhaling the scent of baby powder, Tasha forced away a sharp stab of envy as she held three-month-old Jason Bryant Swain in her arms for the first time. Never again would she hold a baby of her own. And that knowledge formed an ever present ache in her chest she knew would always be there.

Cliff had dropped off Tasha and the children at the Swain ranch house early that morning. She and her sister had visited, waiting until Jason was awake and fed and ready for his day. Meanwhile, Melissa and Stevie had turned the front porch into a makeshift jungle gym, climbing on the railing and leaping off the steps to entertain themselves.

Stroking the baby's soft cheek, Tasha swallowed the raw sense of disappointment at fate's cruel trick. "You did good, big sister."

Ella fussed with Jason's knit cap, motherly pride radiating from her like a lighthouse beacon. "It wasn't all my doing. Bryant contributed a few good genes, too."

"From your glow, I'd guess he's contributing more to your health and welfare than just a few baby genes."

Ella's healthy complexion took on the rosy hue of a woman in love and her eyes filled with mirth behind her big round glasses. "Let's say marriage *and* motherhood agree with me."

A couple of inches shorter than Tasha, her hair a shade or two darker, Ella had always been the smart one in the family. Tasha had spent her adolescence envying her sister's good grades and the respect she'd received from being smart instead of simply pretty. But Ella's hasty marriage last summer to Bryant Swain had startled everyone in the family. Tasha was glad the relationship was working out. A claim she couldn't make about either her too young marriage to Robert Reynolds when she'd learned she was pregnant with Melissa, or her recent botched engagement.

Definitely time for her to swear off men. Her judgment regarding the opposite sex left a lot to be desired.

"We'd better go," Ella said, picking up a light jacket from the back of the couch and slipping it on. "The kids are itching to get out to where they're branding the calves. If we aren't careful, those two are likely to head off on their own."

"All the way from New York, Melissa's been asking when she'd get to see real cowboys."

Ella laughed. "We'll take the truck."

"Thank goodness we don't have to ride a horse."

"I'm not quite ready for that yet."

They went out the back way—leaving the door unlocked, Tasha noted—and called the children around to the side of the house where the truck was parked. Well-kept barns and outbuildings suggested the ranch was a prosperous enterprise, though Ella had said raising cattle was always a risky business financially.

"Learning to ride is one of my goals for this summer," Ella said. "When I get good enough, I may even take up barrel racing."

"Ella! You wouldn't!" Tasha choked on a surprised laugh, but was unable to suppress a ripple of fear that sped through her. "You'll get yourself killed."

Her sister grinned at her. "Well, if not barrel racing, there's a women's mounted drill team. Maybe I could do that instead."

From Tasha's perspective, that didn't sound all that much safer.

Shaking her head, Tasha strapped Jason in his car seat and stood back while Stevie and Melissa clambered into the rear seat of the truck with the baby.

Whatever had gotten into her sister, moving from New York to California and then without warning all the way to Montana? This was a nice enough place to visit for a week or two, no doubt peaceful in a way that would help Tasha put the disappointment of the past few weeks behind her. But she was a city girl. Horses and cows—and all that went with them—weren't her cup of tea.

Still, as she thought of the Swain brothers, she had to admit there was something very appealing about the rugged, outdoor men who lived in the West.

But that didn't mean she was going to get involved with her handsome employer.

Speaking of which, she'd better see if Ella had some recipes she could share. Last night it was pretty obvious tuna sandwiches and soup weren't going to hack it for a man who expended thousands of calories rounding up little doggies all day. And she didn't think her typical salad greens and cottage cheese would cut it, either.

She grinned at the thought. Wouldn't her modeling friends and fashion designer colleagues get a kick out of seeing her now, in jeans and sharkskin boots, bouncing in a pickup along nothing wider than a rutted trail en route to round up a bunch of cows destined to be turned into hand-tooled leather jackets?

DUST AND DIRT rose fifty feet straight up toward a cloudless sky before dissipating in a slight breeze. The noise was astounding—bawling cows, squealing calves and cowboys shouting X-rated obscenities children shouldn't hear. The air reeked of smoke and burning leather.

"Mommy, look what they're doing!" Melissa made a dash for the pen where they were branding the new calves.

Tasha snared her daughter by the back of her jacket. "Oh, no you don't, young lady. Don't you go running off on your own. Those cows will trample you if you're not careful. You are to stay *right* next to me like we're glued together.''

"But, Mommy!" Melissa whined.

Stevie had already raced ahead and was climbing the wooden fence surrounding the pen. "Stevie!" Tasha shrieked, envisioning the boy toppling over and falling beneath the hooves of the agitated animals.

Ella slipped little Jason into a sling across her middle and cuddled her baby next to her. "Stevie will be fine. He knows to stay out of the pen."

Tasha lacked her sister's confidence. The entire scene was as chaotic as the New York theater district right after the Broadway shows released their audiences, spilling them out onto the streets and sidewalks all at once. No one seemed to be in charge of the choreography. Cowboys on horseback darted through the milling herd, ropes twirling over their heads. Clutches of cows and their calves danced back and forth trying to avoid capture and separation. Swirling dust softened the edges of the scene, making it all look surreal. Or nightmarish.

Tasha would sooner make her way through Times Square on New Year's Eve than journey into that chaos.

But Melissa, like an eager puppy on a leash, tugged her forward.

As they approached the fence, Tasha noticed one of the cowboys miss with his lariat, the rope falling harmlessly to the ground. Another cowboy twisted around in his saddle so quickly he nearly unseated himself.

"Watch what you're doing, Shane!" Cliff yelled.

"Ri...ght, boss." The boy's voice cracked.

"Looks like the hands have noticed your arrival," Ella said, amused.

"Next time I'll wear a sack over my head."

"Sis, with your perfect size six figure, it's going to take more than a sack to get these men to ignore you."

Tasha knew she drew the attention of men like pigeons to peanuts. It was both blessing and curse. She needed her looks because of her job, but at heart she was shy and wished—just once—that a man would admire her for something more than an accident of birth.

At least the swearing appeared to have subsided, she thought with relief.

Cliff reined his mount around, exiting the branding pen. He was no better than Shane had been. When Tasha had shown up wearing skintight jeans and a rhinestone-studded denim jacket, he'd almost dropped his teeth along with his lasso. Her langorous walk was sweet, hot sex on the hoof and capable of blowing holes in a man's good sense with every sway of her curvy hips.

He rode to where she and her sister were standing. "Morning, Ella." He tipped his hat to Tasha. She ought to be wearing a hat, too. But then he wouldn't have the pleasure of seeing her white-gold hair held back from her face with a couple of fancy combs and hanging loose down her back. "You two getting reacquainted?"

"It's wonderful to have my sister here," Ella

said, tipping her head back so she could see from beneath her straw hat. "Thanks for looking after her."

"I thought she was supposed to be looking after me."

"Oh, I'm sure she'll do a good job of that, too."

Cliff wasn't quite sure what to make of Ella's quiet, self-satisfied laugh or the gleam in her eyes. Maybe it was just a trick of the sunlight glancing off her glasses.

Straddling the fence, Stevie said, "Can I help you cut out the calves, Dad?"

"Sure you can. I've got Star Song all saddled for you."

"You're going to let him ride into that mess?" Tasha asked, her expression stunned, even a little frightened if Cliff read her right.

He shrugged. "Sure. Someday he'll own part of the Double S."

"But he's only five years old."

"Going on six," the boy corrected, clambering down from the fence.

"I'm almost seven," Melissa said. "Can I help, too?"

"You certainly may not!" Tasha admonished her.

Reaching down, Cliff gripped his son's forearm and hefted him to the back of his horse. "You'll have to wait till you learn how to ride, Melissa. Stevie's been riding since before he could walk."

Melissa's angelic face soured into a pout. "Girls can do all the stuff boys can."

"Sure they can," Cliff agreed. Except Melissa

and her mom weren't likely to stay around long enough for either of them to become good riders. And that reminded Cliff he didn't want Stevie to get too attached to either of them. Sometimes he caught the boy in the master bedroom studying his mother's picture, his expression heart-wrenchingly sad. Cliff didn't want his son to go through another emotional loss like that. Nor did he want to face the bleak sense of abandonment again that had dogged his own life since he and his twin brother were deserted by their biological mother. They'd been about four at the time and he still had a vague recollection of his mother crying.

He circled his horse, coming up beside Tasha, who quickly stepped away from him, placing Melissa safely behind her.

For the moment, Tasha was his housekeeper, and because of his need for child care Cliff had no choice but to treat her as such. Until she decided to move on or he made other arrangements. "I've got to work the four-to-twelve shift tonight. I'll plan to take my dinner break about seven, if that's okay with you." Maybe if he gave her some warning, she'd come up with something more than tuna sandwiches for supper.

"That's fine, but—" She glanced around as if she'd landed on an alien planet. "You mean to tell me you're going to work all day punching cattle, or whatever you call it, then work another eight hours tonight?"

"Yes, ma'am." He thumbed his hat back on his head and added a big dose of drawl to his Western accent. "Can't leave the good folks of Reed County unprotected from rustlers and other varmints just so's I can stay home with a pretty little lady."

She looked up at him slack-jawed.

"My daddy's a deputy sheriff," Stevie explained. "He catches bad guys."

"You got that straight, bucko." Though for the past year a band of rustlers had been operating in the area and neither he nor Sheriff Colman had been able to get a decent lead on them.

"All right. I'll have dinner ready about seven."

"Steak and potatoes would be good," he suggested in the hope of avoiding another batch of tea sandwiches. "And when you've got a minute, Sylvia washed a bunch of my uniform shirts before she left for her daughter's place but didn't have time to iron them. Could you take care of that for me? They're in the laundry room."

That cute little inverted V formed between her eyebrows again. "Anything else you'd like taken care of, Deputy Swain?" she asked tautly.

Yeah, there was something else he'd like, but he wasn't going to go down that path. In fact, he'd be better off if she decided she didn't much like the idea of playing housekeeper, even if she did need the money—a topic they hadn't discussed in any detail yet. Though, come to think of it, Ella knew what Cliff had been willing to pay. She'd probably mentioned the salary to her sister.

"I'll let you know if I think of anything." With that, he tapped his heels to his horse and rode toward the remuda where the string of extra mounts were tethered away from the action.

Tasha blew out a sigh; her jaw ached from clamping her mouth shut instead of coming back at Cliff with a smart remark. "Are all cowboys that chauvinistic?" she asked her sister.

"They tend to be a bit arrogant, which is part of their appeal."

Melissa wrapped her arms around Tasha's waist, hugging her. "What's chuff-in-istic, Mommy?"

"It's when a man thinks all a woman is good for is to cook his meals and wash his clothes."

Ella's laughter rippled through the air, adding a high note to the masculine sounds of the roundup. "Oh, I think Clifford has something else on his mind when he looks at you, Sis, but it's a little too soon for him to pursue that particular activity."

"What's Aunt Ella mean?"

Heat flooded Tasha's cheeks. "Don't ask, sweetheart. Just don't ask." The possibility that Cliff harbored the same sensual thoughts that had plagued Tasha since last night was unsettling. Despite what others might think of her, or how they judged her from her appearance alone, she didn't engage in recreational sex. And developing a deeper relationship with Cliff would be beyond foolish. She was a New Yorker. He was a Montana cowboy. Speaking of which...

"How is it I got the distinct impression from what you told me that Cliff needed a *nanny* for his little boy, not so much a housekeeper? You wouldn't be trying a little matchmaking in your spare time, would you, sister dear?''

''*Moi?* Why, whatever do you mean?''

Tasha glared at her sister. She'd been ambushed, darn it all, and she wasn't going to stand for—

''Morning, missus.'' A bowlegged cowboy had climbed the fence and dropped down beside Ella. He lifted his hat, uncovering a nearly bald head except for a curly fringe of carrot-red hair. Immediately Tasha recognized him from Ella's wedding day—Rusty the ranch foreman.

''Hello, Rusty. Good to see you again,'' Tasha said, extending her hand.

Giving her a big grin, and wiping his hand on his dusty trousers, he shook hands with her. ''Welcome back to Montana, ma'am.''

''Thank you.''

Ella said, ''Rusty's been wonderful to me and Bryant. I don't think the ranch could get along without him. I know I couldn't.''

''You'd do jest fine.'' He peered at the baby cradled in the sling across Ella's chest. ''He's growing like a weed, ain't he? He'll be riding broncs with his daddy in no time, I reckon.''

Tasha shuddered at the thought, though she noted Ella didn't seem disturbed by the possibility of her baby being tossed around on the back of a wild mustang.

''You planning to stay long, ma'am?'' Rusty asked Tasha.

''Not really. In fact, I may cut my trip short.''

The urge to escape Cliff's superheated masculinity was a powerful one.

"You can't," Ella insisted. "How will Cliff run his campaign for sheriff if he doesn't have someone to look after Stevie?"

"*And* fix his meals," Tasha said pointedly.

"Now that boy is a real big eater, that he is," Rusty said.

"Stevie?" Tasha questioned, momentarily confused.

"Nope, Cliff's the one I mean. His brother, too, for that matter. Them two could put away a whole side of beef without any trouble at all when they was teenagers. Quite a sight to behold, it was. Kept their mama hopping in the kitchen, I can tell you that. I remember the time…"

He went on to describe when the adolescent twins had tried to outdo each other at Thanksgiving dinner and had been sick for days afterward. Somewhere in the middle of that story, Shane, the young man whose voice had cracked, joined in the conversation. Another couple of hired hands—Billy Bob and Dingle—sauntered over, happy to make Tasha's acquaintance. A shorter man with a barrel chest wandered in to join the crowd.

Pretty soon Tasha noticed the cows weren't putting up the ruckus they had been earlier. In fact, not much was happening as far as branding was concerned. The cows stood quietly chewing their cuds while the calves nursed or frolicked with their friends.

That was when both Cliff and his brother Bryant

came riding into the midst of the crowd that had gathered around Tasha, cutting the men off as if they were calves being separated from their mothers.

"Gentlemen, you get paid for branding calves, not for chatting up the two prettiest women in the county." Bryant leaned out of his saddle far enough to kiss his wife on the lips.

"What? Not the whole state?" she complained, laughing.

"Haven't seen all the girls in the state yet, and I didn't want to exaggerate."

"Well, don't you go lookin', either, cowboy, or you'll hear from me."

Tasha was stunned by the exchange between husband and wife. Despite her big glasses, simple haircut and minimal makeup, Ella looked truly beautiful...and she'd shown more spark than Tasha could remember seeing in her intellectual sister. Marriage—and the love of a good man—had obviously changed her.

With a sinking heart, Tasha realized she'd very likely never have the chance to experience that kind of happy makeover. She might remain beautiful, though that would be an increasingly difficult battle as she grew older. But she'd never have that glow, the pure radiance Ella had achieved by simply being in love.

Tasha tried to suppress the envy that welled up in her but found she couldn't. Instead, she turned away, her arm hooked over her daughter's shoulder, and headed back toward Ella's truck. She needed to start making calls to agents she knew in New York. She needed to get on with her life.

A few weeks was all she had promised Cliff. Even that might be too long if she wanted to protect her heart.

WHEN TASHA had driven through Reilly's Gulch yesterday, she'd been concentrating more on finding the turnoff to the Double S than to the details of the town. Now, en route to find a grocery store to restock Cliff's pitiful supply of fresh fruit and vegetables—and with the children pouting in the back seat because they had to leave the roundup before the last calf was branded—she cruised slowly down the main street checking out the buildings.

The local elementary school and the adjacent county building had matching flag poles out front, the flags fluttering gently in the afternoon breeze. The Cattlemen's Association occupied a building next to what looked like abandoned railroad tracks.

The small business district didn't look very promising, except for Sal's Hotel, Bar and Grill at the end of the block where several pickups were parked out front. A gas station with repair bays sat opposite a feed store, a mechanic in blue overalls dozing in the sun.

Just as she spotted the grocery store, a red Mazda Miata convertible bumbled out of an alley in front of her and wheeled into the perfect angled parking space right at the door—the one she'd been planning to pull into.

She swore under her breath. The guy must be a

transplanted Manhattan cab driver! At least it wasn't the last spot in the city.

"Mommy, you're not supposed to say bad words," Melissa reminded her.

She glanced at her daughter in the rearview mirror. "You're right, sweetheart. I'll have to put another quarter in our piggy bank when we get back home."

"We're saving up to see *The Nutcracker* at Lincoln Center," Melissa explained to Stevie.

"You wanna eat nuts?"

"No, silly. *The Nutcracker's* a ballet."

Tasha picked a parking spot two slots down from the Mazda and pulled in between a pickup and a Jeep.

"What's a ballet?" Stevie asked as he followed Melissa out of the car.

Melissa did a pirouette on the sidewalk and pranced around on her tiptoes, showing off. Though, given she was wearing jeans and a T-shirt, the dance lacked a true classical flavor without the proper costuming. "Haven't you ever seen a ballet?"

He jammed his hands in his pockets, hanging his head as if he'd missed something important in life. "Uh-uh."

"Mommy, can we take Stevie to a ballet sometime?"

"I don't think Reilly's Gulch has those, honey." A cultural hot spot, it wasn't.

"Well, if it did, could we take him?" Melissa persisted.

"I suppose." Cupping her daughter's shoulder,

she ushered her toward the grocery store and reached out for Stevie's hand, too. "Come on, kids. We've got to get Stevie's daddy something to eat for dinner." And then she was going to have to *iron,* of all things. Hadn't this place heard of dry cleaners? Or wash and wear?

An older gentleman wearing a sporty plaid beret and a frayed suit jacket met her at the grocery store entrance. He tipped his cap to her, revealing thinning white hair, and nodded toward her car.

"Mighty fine lookin' Beamer," he said.

"Thank you." She considered skirting past him, but he was pretty well blocking the center of the double doors.

"That's my Mazda."

Vaguely recalling her sister had owned a Mazda convertible and sold it last winter, Tasha forced a smile. She resisted telling him what she thought of a man who'd steal a parking spot right out from under her nose.

"Red is nice," she said noncommittally.

Aware of the dangers of talking to strangers, Melissa clung to her side.

Stevie charged forward. "Hi, Mr. O'Reilly."

The older man shifted his wrinkles into a glad smile. "Hello, young Steven. Looks like you're escorting two lovely ladies today."

Stevie giggled. "These aren't ladies. She's our new housekeeper." He pointed at Tasha, then indicated Melissa. "And she's only a little girl, same as I'm a little boy."

''You're littler,'' Melissa corrected. ''I'm almost seven.''

Before an argument broke out, Tasha introduced herself to the gentleman, who she learned was Chester O'Reilly, descendant of the town founders, and the owner of the only franchised taxi service in Reilly's Gulch. She thought the reason for only one such service in town was pretty obvious, but he seemed so proud of his community duties, Tasha didn't see any reason to point out the probable lack of demand for cabs in this small town.

As she tried to excuse herself to get on with her shopping, he said, ''If you decide to sell your Beamer, let me know. I'm thinking of expanding my taxi service.''

''You are?'' That sounded like the height of optimism to Tasha.

''Yep. Billy Flynn turned over his ranch operations to his boys and he's got some extra time on his hands. Figured I could keep him busy doing taxi work. Shoot, he's only eighty-two, way too young to retire. And there's lots of potential 'round here, you know. Only a question of time till I'm busier than flies on a fresh cow pie.''

''Yes, well...'' She wrinkled her nose and mumbled something about keeping Chester in mind if she decided to sell her car while she was in town, then scooted herself and the children past him into the grocery store.

Reilly's Gulch might lack for cultural amenities but the town certainly wasn't short on characters.

Tasha suspected Chester was only the tip of that particular iceberg.

She doubted the town was short of good-looking men, either. Unfortunately one in particular held a special attraction for her.

Clifford Swain.

Chapter Three

Cliff pulled his truck into the sheriff's parking lot behind the combined city hall and county courthouse, a squat brick building that had been constructed in the 1930s. He'd barely had time to stop by home, shower and get dressed after his day at the roundup. He'd given Stevie a hug, said a quick hello to Tasha and her daughter, and then he'd been on his way.

Fortunately it was only a couple of weeks out of the year when he burned the candle at both ends, being both cowboy and deputy sheriff. But he owned half the Double S. Even though he never took any of the profits from the ranch—assuming there were any—he couldn't leave his brother to do all the hard work during roundups. Besides, he kind of liked keeping his hand in the business.

Aching muscles or not, it felt good to ride hard, work harder and have something to show for his efforts.

Which was more than he could say for the success of the sheriff's office at catching the band of rustlers who'd been plaguing the area for the past year, including the time Cliff was living in Los Angeles.

Adjusting his sidearm, he went into the office. Sheriff Colman was behind the counter talking to Deputy Andy Linear, a Barney Fife look-alike and not a whole lot smarter.

"Afternoon, gentlemen," he said. He hooked his hat on a peg and joined them at the counter where they were studying a large-scale map of the area.

Reed County encompassed some twenty thousand square miles of mostly rolling hills, grassland suitable for grazing cattle. Periodically rivers and winter creeks bisected the land, creating ravines and forming lakes and ponds. To the west, the land rose, becoming more forested. To the east was prairie country. Within the county boundaries only a few small towns existed, shown on the map as clusters of houses and often connected by nothing more than gravel roads.

"What's up?" Cliff asked.

Larry Colman tapped the map at a spot south of Reilly's Gulch. "Got a report of another truckload of steers picked up from the King place last night. The King ranch got hit last year, too."

Larry had put on a good fifty pounds in the years he'd served as county sheriff. Though his body wasn't as agile as it used to be, his mind was still alert and he was eager to get on with retirement in order to pursue his other interests—primarily opening a museum to house his old-time radio memorabilia, from Captain Midnight decoder rings to a set of broadcast tapes from early Green Hornet shows.

"You find tire tracks?" Cliff asked.

"Yep. We went out to investigate this morning first thing. An eighteen wheeler's, rear inside left tire with a notch in it same as the other jobs."

"And another full moon last night," Andy pointed out.

Cliff studied the map. "That's when they do their best work." Last month during the full moon a ranch to the east had been victimized in the same way, the first rustling activity reported since the winter snows had melted. "Looks like it's going to be another long summer unless we get a lead on them. Or they make a mistake."

"These particular crooks are sneaky devils," Larry commented. "Using a big truck like that, then poof! It vanishes into nowhere before we even get word of the missing steers."

Andy said, "It's just like that big TV magician who makes the Statue of Liberty and airplanes and stuff disappear. Now you see it, now you don't."

Cliff suspected they were hiding the truck somewhere safe between jobs, but he didn't have a clue where that might be. So far the Double S hadn't lost any steers. Idly he wondered how long their good luck would last.

The office door opened and in marched Winifred Bruhn, editor, publisher and sole reporter for the *Reed County Register*. She was also a member of the school board and the self-appointed head of the town's morality police.

"Seems to me you folks ought to be out catching criminals instead of standing there chewing the fat." She whipped out a notepad and slapped it on the counter. "Now then, Sheriff, what are you planning to do about those rustlers stealing the livelihoods right out from under our citizens' noses?"

Larry exhaled a long-suffering sigh. "We're working on it, Winnie. Like always."

"Fine lot of good you're doing. How many head were taken last night?" Something about her narrow nose and drooping eyebrows gave her a perpetually sour expression that made it easy to understand why she'd never married. Her shrill voice alone would be enough to scare away any man.

"The Kings figure about thirty," Larry told her.

Winnie jotted that fact down in her notebook.

Having no interest in Winifred's interrogation of the sheriff, Cliff eased away from the counter. The rustlers could be hiding their truck in a whole different county—hell, a different state, for that matter. If they had something more to go on, they could ask other jurisdictions to keep an eye out for the suspect vehicle. As it was, any truck going down the highway could be the one involved in the crime. But they couldn't stop them all to check the tires. Not without probable cause.

Finished with Larry, Winifred cornered Cliff as he was riffling through Wanted flyers. "I want to know what you plan to do about the band of rustlers if you're elected sheriff."

"I'm likely to be elected," he said easily, "since I'm running unopposed."

''That might change. There's another two days left before the filing deadline, young man, and there's talk in town of wanting new blood in the sheriff's office.''

''Sorry to hear that, ma'am.''

''Well, you'd best come up with a statement saying how you plan to catch those crooks. There's folks in this county saying they won't stand for another do-nothing sheriff.''

Irritated by Winifred's criticism of Larry—who'd been a damn good sheriff—Cliff struggled to come up with a decent quote. Of course he planned to catch the rustlers. But in his business there were no guarantees. The voters shouldn't ask for them, but he supposed they had the right, even when that wasn't a fair way to make a judgment. All he could promise was to do his very best.

After what seemed like ages, Winifred left, her notebook filled with misquotes, Cliff was sure. Dealing with the *Reed County Register* and its star reporter wasn't going to be the favorite part of his job as sheriff.

He was just getting ready to go out on patrol when Larry said, ''Looks like you've got a new housekeeper.''

Cliff froze. Had the word already spread he had a cover model working for him—temporarily? ''Where'd you hear that?''

''Didn't.'' Larry got a Santa Claus twinkle in his eyes. ''Whoever ironed your shirt scorched a big triangle right smack in the middle. Figured Sylvia wasn't the culprit.''

Practically dislocating both his neck and his shoulder in order to look at his back, Cliff cursed. Why him? Why couldn't some other man have been in line when they passed out an incompetent housekeeper, one who just happened to be the sexiest female this side of the Mississippi?

One who was definitely double trouble.

CLIFF CAME HOME on his dinner break and Tasha couldn't decide if he looked sexiest dressed in jeans and a work shirt with his Stetson tipped back on his head at a rakish angle, or in his khaki sheriff's uniform, tailored to fit his broad shoulders and narrow waist. Difficult decision, she thought as she watched him wash up at the kitchen sink.

"Hey, Daddy, what's that on the back of your shirt?" Stevie asked. Sitting at the table opposite Melissa, his little legs were swinging back and forth expending nervous energy.

Cliff dried his hands with a towel. "Somebody was using an iron that was too hot."

"Actually, I got distracted when Melissa fell off the porch swing and was screaming bloody murder."

"Stevie pushed me," Melissa said.

"Did not."

Melissa held up her elbow. "I got an owie, Uncle Cliff. Wanna see?"

Tasha contemplated the back of Cliff's shirt as he bent over to examine the Snoopy bandage. "It doesn't look too bad."

"I think she'll live," Cliff said. In an easy gesture

of affection, he brushed a quick kiss to Melissa's elbow.

Tasha's heart squeezed tight at the sight of his gentle caring. Just the way a father should be, except Melissa had never really known her daddy. "No, I meant your shirt."

Eyeing her, Cliff took his place at the head of the table. "I'll change after we eat. It's an old Western custom that we don't wear scorched shirts out in public, particularly when we may have to make an arrest. If the crooks get too many laughs, it makes them unruly."

She flipped her hair behind her shoulder. "Who knows? You might start a new fad."

A reluctant smile played around the corners of his mouth, and she noticed what really nice lips he had—not so full that he'd give sloppy kisses, but pleasantly soft, a shape hers could easily mold to. And that was a thought she shouldn't be considering.

"Are we going to eat anytime soon?" he asked.

She gazed at his mouth for another long heartbeat, thinking—

"Mommy? You aren't going to burn the dinner, are you?"

"No! Absolutely not." Whirling, she grabbed a hot pad, opened the oven door and pulled out the chicken and rice casserole she'd been keeping warm. Not burned. A little dried around the edges maybe but no charcoal.

With a degree of pride, she put the casserole on the table and produced a big bowl of salad from the refrigerator. All the grocery store in town carried was iceberg lettuce and a little wilted Romaine—nothing resembling endive or alfalfa sprouts—but she'd chopped a half-dozen fresh veggies into the mix. Definitely nutritious.

Cliff ladled some of the casserole onto her plate, and she held up her hand to stop him from serving her too much. Then he served Melissa and Stevie.

"I thought we were having steak tonight." He piled several spoonfuls on his own plate, no doubt relieved to see she'd made an adequate quantity to fill up a hardworking cowboy.

"Chicken's better for you. The children, too."

"Better not let the folks around here hear you say that. Those are fightin' words in cattle country."

She met his teasing blue eyes with a wink of her own. "I'll be sure to keep my radical N'Yawker ideas to myself."

As they ate dinner, the children were eager to relate their afternoon activities, which had included Stevie giving Melissa and Tasha a tour of the corral and barn. They'd met Peaches, the aging mare Cliff had apparently decided would be placid enough for Tasha to ride. Henry, the mule, appeared less tranquil, had big yellow teeth and a disposition that would make Manhattan's pushiest panhandlers keep their distance.

"You catch any bad guys today?" Stevie finally asked.

"Not so far." He forked the last of the rice on his plate into his mouth and eyed the remains in the casserole dish.

Tasha gestured for him to help himself to more.

"Ricky Monroe says there's bank robbers 'n murderers 'n aliens all over the place."

He reached over to ruffle his son's hair. "Not in our town, bucko. You're safe here."

Smiling at the boy, Tasha said, "I'd say your friend Ricky has a vivid and rather gory imagination."

"He says he's seen 'em," Stevie insisted.

"Well, if they come around here, they'll have to watch out for me, won't they?" Cliff patted the badge on his chest.

Tasha's unwilling gaze shifted to his holstered weapon and she shuddered. She didn't like guns. Or violence. And wondered how a man who was so obviously gentle could make his living carrying a gun.

Before he could finish off the casserole, he got a call on the radio he had strapped to his belt. An accident on the state highway east of Brady.

"Gotta go, kids." Standing, he gave his son a quick kiss. "Do what Tasha tells you, okay?"

"I will, Daddy."

He circled the table to give Melissa a kiss on the top of her head. "You, too, Little Miss Goldilocks."

She giggled. "I have to. She's my mommy."

For a heart-stopping moment, Tasha thought he was going to kiss her, too. A husband and father going off to work. But then he stopped himself.

"Good dinner...considering the main course used to wear feathers."

She laughed with him, but somewhere deep inside

disappointment curled painfully through her. The family image they'd all created sitting around the kitchen table wasn't real; he hadn't kissed her.

It was hard to tell which one of those truths hurt the most. Although she recognized neither of them should.

CLIFF GOT BACK HOME after midnight and he was bone-weary. The accident near Brady hadn't been too bad, only minor injuries, but it had taken him a long time to complete the paperwork after the tow truck had cleaned up the debris.

He slipped into the house through the back door, sensing the good kind of quiet that meant everything was all right. Smiling, he realized Tasha had left a light on for him in the living room. But he wasn't prepared for what he found there.

She was curled with her legs under her, her head resting on the back of the couch, her hair feathering around her face. On the end table there was an open paperback book as though she'd just laid it down. She had one hand on his son, who was sleeping with his head on her lap, a light blanket arranged over his small form.

Tears stung at the backs of Cliff's eyes. It should have been his wife Yvonne comforting Stevie against whatever fear had kept him awake. But it was another woman. A woman so classically beautiful, she took his breath away. He didn't want to care about her, be attracted to her. Yet every instinct in his body contradicted what he kept telling himself. When it came to Tasha Papadakis Reynolds, he seemed incapable of rational thought.

He knelt beside her. Against his will, his fingers toyed with the ends of her hair—molten silver so fine, it must have been created by the gods.

In sleep, her lips were relaxed, inviting a kiss. Her lashes formed golden half circles beneath her eyes. A splash of color highlighted her cheeks, the makeup so subtle he wasn't sure if what he saw was her natural color or something a brush created. And her sultry scent was all around her, enticing him.

Slowly, as if she were Sleeping Beauty awakening, her eyes opened. Blue magic the shade of midnight.

"Hi." She blinked and ran her tongue across her lips.

He felt the gesture as powerfully as if she'd slid the zipper down on his trousers. "Hi, yourself."

She roused slowly. "You're home safe."

"Hmm. No bad guys out there tonight." Only traffic victims who shouldn't have been driving so fast. "Stevie have a problem?"

"The alien space monsters were after him."

He nodded. "It's that Monroe kid. He's in Stevie's kindergarten class, or was. School's out now."

"Your son seems particularly sensitive."

To Cliff's surprise, she lifted her hand and placed it on his cheek, her fingers incredibly soft and caressing. Delicate like the wings of a butterfly.

"Like his dad, I suspect." She breathed the words as warmly as a summer breeze.

Cliff knew he had to move away—away from her touch. Away from the feelings that swept through him. He'd been lonely for so damn long....

By sheer force of will, he stood. It wouldn't be right for any of them if he followed his impulse to kiss her, to carry her into the guest bedroom and make love to her for the rest of the night.

Instead, he picked his son up in his arms. "Thanks for taking care of my boy."

She gave him a lazy smile. "No problem. That's my job."

For now. She'd be leaving within weeks, maybe even days. They hadn't even worked out the details and Stevie wasn't her responsibility. Cliff didn't want his son hurt when Tasha left. Keeping an emotional distance was better for all concerned.

She followed him into Stevie's bedroom, where she pulled up the covers that Melissa had tossed aside.

Stevie muttered something unintelligible as Cliff tucked him in, then rolled to his side, curled into a ball, instantly falling back into deep sleep.

The night-light cast an orange glow in the room, enough to see the usual clutter had been straightened, the toy box lid closed, the wooden train set in its place on the brightly painted play table Cliff had constructed for Stevie's second birthday, when he'd still had his mother.

Cliff lifted his eyes, meeting Tasha's gaze. The room felt strangely warm, the air sultry with her seductive perfume. She stood on one side of the room, the twin beds between them. Yet he could almost feel the heat of her body touching him.

"Where's Melissa's father?" he asked quietly.

"I have no idea. Our marriage, such as it was, only lasted two years. He said he needed to find himself. The last I heard he was looking in Australia."

Cliff couldn't imagine walking out on his child— or on a wife like Tasha, for that matter.

"This guy you were engaged to…was Melissa upset when you broke it off?"

"Just the opposite." With a quick check of her child, Tasha left her bedside, moving closer to Cliff as soundlessly as a moonbeam. "Nick wasn't very fond of kids. She picked up on that right away, which should have given me a clue that he wasn't exactly the best catch of the year."

"Love can do funny things to people."

She glanced away from him. "I'm not sure love was involved—for either of us. More like convenience, although I admit there was some sexual chemistry. He was my agent and business manager. We often traveled together. It was, well, easy to get involved. It was also a mistake."

He'd like to be able to console her, but that would be a mistake, too.

With a shake of his head, he cleared the image of holding her in his arms. "Morning comes early around here. We'd better call it a night."

"More roundups tomorrow?"

"One more day and we ought to have it licked. For this season."

"Good night, then." She slipped past him, heading for the guest room.

He inhaled her lingering scent, and cursed himself for wanting to follow her all the way to her bed.

HE'D JUST POURED his first cup of morning coffee, and the mug froze halfway to his mouth when Tasha walked into the kitchen. No woman had a right to look that good first thing in the morning—her hair sleep-mussed, her face free of makeup and her cheeks naturally flushed.

Darn it all, he'd like to see her sleepy-eyed, her hair mussed from a night of *his* lovemaking—an image that had kept him awake most of the night. *Not gonna happen,* he reminded himself.

"I heard you up." Pulling her cotton robe modestly around her, she smiled a lazy greeting. "Should I wake the children?"

He tried to act natural, as if he were used to having a beautiful woman in his kitchen every morning. "No, let 'em sleep. If they want to come out to the ranch later, you can bring them."

"Fine." Barefoot, her toenails an intriguing raspberry red, she glided to the coffeepot and poured herself a mug.

"You know how to find the place now?"

"Ella showed me what to look for at the turnoff. Evidently that new invention called street signs hasn't reached Reed County yet."

"We're a little backward," he admitted, taking a gulp of coffee. It burned as it slid down his throat.

"But then, only strangers would need signs, and we don't get many tourists."

"Really? The countryside is beautiful, in its fashion. Reed County must be a well-kept secret." Glancing around the kitchen, she asked, "Do my housekeeping duties include making you breakfast?"

"I've already got the oatmeal on."

She wrinkled her nose. "I'll do toast. Thanks, anyway."

He nodded toward the toaster on the counter. "Help yourself." Getting down a bowl from the cupboard, he stirred the oatmeal.

Someone knocked on the back door.

Cliff swiveled his head that direction, dismayed to find Winifred Bruhn staring at him through the door's window. Not waiting for an invitation, she marched right into the kitchen.

"Now, isn't this a cozy domestic scene!" Her gray hair was frazzled and windblown, her omnipresent notebook in her hand.

He leveled her his harshest look, which didn't seem to faze her. "You're supposed to wait until someone says come in after you knock." Her sudden arrival had startled him so badly, he'd nearly dropped the damn pot of oatmeal on the floor.

"Pshaw! I can't wait on folks when I've got a newspaper deadline to meet." She looked Tasha up and down with the eye of a predator—or someone about to make an arrest on behalf of the morality police. "I don't believe I've had the pleasure of meeting this young lady."

Impatient, and angered by the woman's unspoken insinuations, Cliff made perfunctory introductions. "What do you want, Winnie?"

"You say she's your housekeeper?" she asked, busily scribbling notes that would no doubt appear in the local gossip column. And probably be vicious in the conclusions drawn.

"Would you like some coffee, Ms. Bruhn?" Tasha asked smoothly, though a blush had risen to her cheeks.

"She doesn't have time for coffee. She has a deadline to meet, right, Winnie?"

The woman lifted her nose, sniffing with an air of superiority. "I've come by to tell you Bobby Bruhn has decided to run against you for sheriff. I'd like a statement—"

"Bobby? He doesn't have any law enforcement experience. What makes him think—"

"I assure you, the full weight and influence of the *Reed County Register* will be behind Mr. Bruhn's election."

"He's your nephew, for crying out loud!"

"It's time for a change in this county, a breath of fresh air. Now I can print your reaction to Mr. Bruhn's candidacy or I can indicate, despite the efforts of the press to gain an interview, you were otherwise engaged...." She eyed Tasha pointedly. "And that you had no comment. The choice is yours, Deputy Swain."

Chapter Four

Cliff's hands balled into fists. He'd never in his life hit a woman. He wasn't going to start now with this nosy busybody. He'd get a bad reputation with the electorate as well as violate his own personal code of conduct. But damn! He'd really like the chance to—

"I'm sure Deputy Swain welcomes all challengers," Tasha said, stepping forward as though she dealt with the press every day of her life, even when caught in her bathrobe and without her makeup. "And he has confidence in the wisdom of the voters to make the best possible decision for the county and its residents. Isn't that right, Mr. Swain?"

"Uh, yeah, that's perfect. Write that down, Winnie."

Winifred scowled; her pencil didn't budge. "I think I'd rather hear it from the candidate himself."

"Okay." Feeling a little more in control, he leaned back against the kitchen counter. "I welcome all challengers and I'm confident the voters will make the right decision for the county. Now, did you get that?''

She harrumphed, but finally scribbled something on her notepad. ''Your campaign won't be a walk-over, young man, not with the *Register* backing your opponent,'' she warned.

As if anyone read the paper for more than news of 4H activities. ''I'm confident the voters will—''

She waved off the repetition of his official comment. ''With a well-funded candidate in the running against you, you can be sure the voters will ask you to defend your record, along with Sheriff Colman's. At candidates' meetings you'll have to speak for yourself.''

''No problem.'' Shoving away from the counter, he intentionally moved into her personal space. She smelled powerfully of some cheap perfume. ''Didn't you say you have a deadline?''

She backed up a step. ''You can't intimidate—''

''Goodbye, Winnie. Happy reporting.'' Using his size and a bad-cop expression, he ushered her to the back door. From now on he'd better start locking the damn thing. Winifred Bruhn gave new meaning to the expression *home invasion*.

When he turned around, he found Tasha looking pale and shaken. ''That was a great quote. Thanks,'' he said.

''I've put you in a difficult position, haven't I?''

Uncomfortable with the idea of Winnie spreading vicious rumors about him or Tasha, he avoided looking directly at her. ''Naw, Winnie likes to blow smoke, is all. Nobody in their right mind would vote for her nephew. He's about as sleazy as they come.''

''But if people don't know him—''

''Most do.''

She set her mug on the counter. ''I think Melissa and I ought to stay with my sister—''

''What about Stevie?''

''You'll find someone else to watch out for him. My being here is just going to add fuel to the newspaper's campaign against you. That Winifred person has a bee in her bonnet and she's determined—''

In three strides he crossed the kitchen, taking Tasha by the shoulders. She felt delicate in his hands. Fragile. And he had the urge to protect her from Winnie and anyone else who wanted to attack her—physically or personally.

''Look, we haven't done anything wrong. You're filling in for my housekeeper. Hell, you're a relative doing a favor for me. It's as simple as that. And I won't back down because some two-bit reporter wants to make more of what she saw here than really exists.'' He struggled not to think about *wanting* more. That had never been in the cards. Not with Tasha planning to return to New York within weeks. ''The fact is, with Bobby Bruhn running, I'll need you more than ever to watch after Stevie. You can bet there'll be candidate meetings in every little town in the county. And Kiwanis luncheons, women's club tea parties. They'll have me running from one end of this county to another. If you're not here, what am I going to do with Stevie?''

"There must be someone..." Her eyes filled with concern, blue and tempting.

"I've asked around. Given my work hours, there aren't many women who'll either move in here for six weeks or run back and forth between their house and mine at all times of the day and night. It just doesn't work out real well." Forget only yesterday he'd vowed to find someone else. Now, Winnie had gotten his back up. He didn't like being forced into a corner.

"No, I suppose it's difficult to find someone like that."

"So you'll stay?"

"Six weeks? I'd hoped by then I'd have a new agent."

"Stay as long as you can. Meanwhile I'll fight off Winnie and her small-town tabloid journalism."

She seemed to study his face. He couldn't imagine what she saw, but he desperately wanted her to say yes. At the same time he knew there would be risks that had nothing to do with a political campaign.

"All right," she said softly, her voice like a physical caress. "I'll stay—until I find a new agent who lands me a decent assignment."

He exhaled slowly, the weight of anticipation easing from his shoulders. She'd stay awhile. That was all he could ask—and more than he should want.

"YOU'RE THAT WOMAN who's living with Cliff Swain, aren't you?"

Tasha bristled as she helped Stevie climb into the

barber chair for a haircut. Trust the news to have reached the combined beauty-and-barber shop in Reilly's Gulch before it made headlines in the weekly newspaper.

"I'm filling in for his housekeeper," she said, wondering how many times she'd have to tell people before they'd believe nothing was going on between her and Cliff. Or when she'd believe it herself. There was something very intimate about living in the same house with a man as potently masculine as Cliff. In the three days she'd been there, the feeling hadn't dimmed one whit. It had almost been a relief when he'd asked her to bring Stevie in for a haircut while he did some work around the house. Melissa had insisted upon staying home with him.

"I'm Candy McCloud and that's Harriet—she owns the shop," the dark-haired beautician announced, indicating an older woman who was dying a customer's hair. The woman in the chair looked to be as large as a football player and had big meaty arms. "And that's Sal from across the street."

Tasha nodded hello, guessing the woman was the owner of Sal's Bar and Grill and probably handled the bouncer duties on her own.

Candy draped Stevie with a cloth smock and gave him a quick smile. "Cliff and I went to school together. Bryant, too, of course. Those boys were something else, I'll tell you. By eighth grade, every girl in town had a crush on them."

Tasha forced a pleasant smile, the one she used when a photo assignment had been going on too long.

"Yvonne was the one who caught him, though. He never had eyes for anybody else. Still doesn't, and don't you know we single girls in town have all tried. Why only last month—"

"Candy!" Sal boomed. "Will you quit your yammering and get to cuttin' that little boy's hair. Nobody 'round here is interested in a blow-by-blow of your version of *The Young and the Restless*."

Unfazed by Sal's comment, Candy said to Stevie, "How short do you want it, honey? Anything special this time?"

Stevie lifted his small shoulders beneath the drape. "What you usually do, I guess."

"Not too short," Tasha suggested. "I don't want him to look like he's been skinned."

"Whatever you say." Snipping her scissors in the air a few times—apparently to warm up to the real thing—she began to trim Stevie's hair. "You know, hon," she said to Tasha, "you look kind of familiar. Are you somebody famous or something?"

Tasha took a chair to watch the activities. "I'm Ella Swain's sister. There's probably a family resemblance."

"Ella's my aunt," Stevie said. "She makes real good cookies."

"That a fact?" Sal said, her dark eyes brightening with interest. "Ella's a good friend of mine. She does my books, bless her heart. I can't abide all that detail work and I sure 'n heck can't tell a debit from a credit. Besides, all that paperwork used to interfere with my soaps. Now Ella just lets me know that I've still got money in the bank."

"I'm glad she's able to help you out." Certainly Tasha didn't have the brains to handle anything more than the simplest accounting project—her checkbook was about it. She wasn't too swift when it came to baking, either.

"Yep, for a greenhorn, that sister of yours sure ran Bryant around in circles till he stood still long enough to get lassoed." Sal grinned at her in the mirror. "Smart girl, she is, the independent sort a woman like me can appreciate."

"They seem very happy together."

"Don't suppose you're lookin' to hook up with Cliff? Sorta keep things in the family?"

A flush stole up Tasha's cheeks. "I'm really just on a break between jobs. New York's my home. I won't be staying here long."

"Pity. Cliff could use a good woman, too."

Candy, who'd obviously been following the conversation, continued to study Tasha even as she clipped Stevie's hair. "You know, I really think I've seen you—"

Scissors still in hand, she wandered over to the end table between the two hair dryers and flipped through the magazines piled helter-skelter there.

"I knew it!" Candy held up her trophy, a copy of the fashion magazine with Tasha on the cover. "This is you, isn't it, hon? Right here on the front of this magazine."

"Well, I'll be damned," Sal said. She spun her chair around to get a better look, almost knocking Harriet off her feet.

Harriet took the magazine from Candy. "Oh,

aren't you a pretty thing. What brand of hair coloring do you use?''

''Only a cream rinse to bring out the natural color,'' Tasha assured them, for the first time not all that pleased with being a cover model. In New York there was a fair amount of anonymity, even when you made the cover of a magazine. Certainly she was small potatoes compared to the celebrities who spent time in Manhattan. In Reilly's Gulch, Tasha would be something of a freak. She wasn't at all sure she liked the attention. Nor was she confident her notoriety wouldn't hurt Cliff's election campaign.

While Candy, Harriet and Sal were fussing over the magazine, the shop door opened and in came an adolescent boy with a bag of newspapers slung over his shoulder. He tossed one on the counter, leaving without comment.

From across the room, Tasha read the bold headline: Candidate For Sheriff In Questionable Relationship.

SHE WAS STILL thoroughly annoyed by the newspaper article and headline when she got back to Cliff's place, and then she almost died at what she saw.

''Look, Aunt Tasha! Melissa's riding my horse!'' Stevie nearly flew out of the car as soon as it came to a stop.

Tasha's heart had stopped beating. ''Oh, my God!''

Melissa looked so small, so vulnerable on top of

the massive animal. Forget Cliff held the bridle, walking the horse around the corral. The mere sight of her only child riding a horse sent an explosion of panic through Tasha. She'd never be able to survive if something awful happened to her baby.

Be cool, she told herself as she got out of the car. Cliff would think she was a total ninny if he realized how afraid she was of horses.

Stevie had already raced to the corral, climbing up the fence and perching himself on top. He didn't seem concerned Melissa was riding his horse, just delighted his father had brought the animal back from the main ranch after the roundup had been completed.

Tasha followed more slowly, her stomach knotted, her legs unsteady.

Meanwhile Melissa's grin was about as wide as the expanse from Montana to New York, and she waved with her free hand—the hand she should have been holding on with. "Hi, Mommy. Look at me."

"I'm looking, sweetie." Though, like viewing a scary movie, Tasha would rather have covered her eyes.

"You ready to try it by yourself, short stuff?" Cliff asked.

"Isn't it a little soon for her to be on her own?" Tasha blurted out the plea before she could stop herself.

Melissa would have none of her mother's overprotection. "I can do it," she insisted.

Cliff released his grip on the horse.

Tasha thought she was going to be sick. The image of the horse trampling Melissa in the same way a horse had knocked her down and almost trampled her rose up in Tasha's imagination. She had to clamp her hand over her mouth to prevent a scream. God, she never should have brought Melissa to Montana.

"Remember not to tug on the reins," Cliff said. "Guide her gently and let Star Song do all the work."

He stood back as Melissa and the horse circled the corral.

Stevie shouted his encouragement. "You're doing good."

Spots swam in front of Tasha's eyes, and she realized she was holding her breath. She exhaled slowly, carefully.

"One more time around the loop, Melissa, and it'll be your mother's turn."

"No!"

Cliff turned, startled by Tasha's emphatic refusal. She was standing outside the corral, her face chalky white, her hands gripping the top rail of the fence. From the way her eyes were glazed, Cliff thought that if she let go, she'd fall down. She looked as if she'd gone into shock.

"Hey, what's wrong?"

She shook her head. "Nothing."

He climbed the fence and dropped down beside her.

"Don't leave Melissa alone in there with that animal."

"She'll be fine. Even if she drops the reins, Star Song will simply come to a stop. She's as gentle as a..."

"Please...."

Seeing how terrified Tasha was, Cliff cupped her face, soothing his hand over her velvety skin. He ignored his own reactions, the hot flow of blood to his lower regions, determined to find out what was wrong. "Tell me what's goin' on, Goldilocks," he urged quietly.

"It's silly."

"I don't think so, not the way you're acting."

For a moment she took her eyes off of Melissa and looked at him. Fear had turned her eyes to navy blue. "I'm afraid of horses." She licked her lips. "Desperately afraid."

"Okay. Do you know why you're so afraid?"

"Of course I do. I'm not crazy. Just...chicken."

He repressed a smile. "I know you're not crazy. How 'bout telling me what happened?"

"It was a long time ago." Her eagle eye was on Melissa and Star Song again, as though she expected one or the other to bolt. "Mother had taken us to the theater and we were walking home through Central Park. There was a protest, a near riot, hundreds of people. I have no idea what it was all about."

She began to tremble. Instinctively, Cliff pulled her into his arms. Though tall, her eyes almost meeting his, there was something delicate about her. Something fragile.

"What's wrong with Aunt Tasha?" Stevie asked.

"She's just remembering some bad stuff that happened when she was a kid. You keep an eye on Melissa for me. Okay, son?''

Tasha seemed to steady herself, but Cliff didn't let her go. The combination of her sultry, tropical scent and her fears acted on him like an aphrodisiac. Despite the poor timing, he wanted to keep her close.

''Go on,'' he urged. Tendrils of her hair had escaped their clip, and he swept them back from the column of her neck, knowing at another time, in another place, he'd kiss her there.

''The mounted police came into the park, pushing people back. Mother tried to pull us out of the way. I fell down.'' She squeezed her eyes shut. ''All I could see were the horse's hooves. I thought—''

''Shh, sweetheart,'' he soothed. ''You're okay now. And I promise I won't let anything bad happen to Melissa.''

Her eyes flashed open and searched the corral for her daughter. ''She's all right, isn't she? I mean, the horse—''

''You've got nothing to worry about. Not with Melissa on Star Song. Now, when she's a teenager and the boys get a good look at her, that's a whole different story.''

She tried for a weak smile. ''You must think I'm the silliest mother in the whole world.''

''Nope. You were traumatized by a horse that you thought was going to step on you. It's understandable you're a little skittery around them yourself and worried about Melissa. But trust me, by the time you leave Montana, you'll be riding a horse like an ol' pro yourself.'' He grinned at her. ''And that's a promise.''

''Oh, no.'' She shook her head, the fear in her eyes flaring again. ''Allowing Melissa to experience riding a horse—*inside* a corral—is one thing. But there's no way *I'm* going to get up on top of one of those beasts myself. Absolutely no way.''

Cliff loved a challenge, he always had. Tasha represented that and a whole lot more. He simply didn't know if she'd stick around long enough for him to actually keep his promise.

Drawing herself up to her full five-foot-nine height and backing away from Cliff, she said, ''Isn't that enough for Melissa's first lesson?''

''Sure. I'll get her.''

''Oh, and I brought home a copy of this week's *Reed County Register* from the beauty shop. I don't think you'll be pleased by what that woman wrote about us.''

''I'll check it out later.'' Giving her a concerned look, he agilely climbed back over the fence, crossing the corral to take Star Song in hand again.

TASHA MADE SURE Melissa was off the horse and safely *outside* the corral before she went into the house.

Feeling on edge, she put on one of her own CDs, listening while she tried to decide what to cook for dinner. Next time she was in town she'd have to convince the owner of the grocery store to carry a selection of ready-made pasta salads. The results might not be like having a New York deli close at hand, but it would be a step in the right direction. Although the thought didn't distract her from what was really making her tense.

Her surging adrenaline when she'd seen Melissa on that horse must have been the reason she'd reacted so strongly to Cliff holding her. She'd wanted to bury her face at the crook of his neck, stand there crying in his arms until her fears went away. She'd wanted him to kiss her.

As Andrea Bocelli's romantic tenor voice soared through the house, she decided she wanted much more than a kiss from Cliff.

She froze in front of the cupboard, her hand on a can of string beans, desire sizzling through her veins. Deep inside her body, she felt a clenching, a tight ache only Cliff could ease.

What on earth was she thinking? She'd only known him for three days. She'd just extricated herself from one relationship. It was far too soon to begin another one. A brief fling would be the height of folly. She wouldn't be here long enough to—

He burst in the back door and halted abruptly. "What on earth is that caterwauling? I thought you had a sick cow in here." He gave her a teasing grin.

It took her a moment to reorient herself and then take offense at his comment. "He happens to be the best tenor in the whole world *and* the most romantic."

Taking off his hat, he hung it on a peg by the door and shook his head. "Let's say I'm more into country and western than opera. You haven't lived till you've danced to Faith Hill."

She raised her brows doubtfully.

Turning away, she added the knowledge that their musical tastes were totally incompatible to the growing list of reasons why she shouldn't have an affair with Clifford Swain. Which didn't reduce the liquid heat that had pooled in her belly the moment he'd walked in the door.

With an amused shrug, Cliff picked up the *Register* Tasha had left on the table and read Winnie's article. Since the kids were outside and well out of hearing, he allowed himself the pleasure of calling Winifred a name he wouldn't want the children to hear.

"You're right," Tasha agreed, glancing over her shoulder. "So, what are you going to do about it?"

"Nothing." The fact that Winifred had insinuated he and Tasha were sleeping together—playing house instead of keeping house—was impossible to contradict without making a huge issue of the whole thing. For the most part, nobody in Reed County cared about what the newspaper said, anyway. "If I come to the defense of your honor, Winnie will just write another article, which would be even more scathing. This kind of gossip is better left alone."

"You're right that my honor doesn't need defending. I don't have to live in this town. But what about your election? Isn't it going to make people question—"

"They can question all they like, and the answer is still no, we haven't done anything wrong." Though admittedly he'd like to do something that seemed absolutely *right,* which could easily be translated as something consenting adults shouldn't be doing in a small town like Reilly's Gulch. Though most of them did it every chance they got.

His gaze fell on another article on the front page, right below the news that Reilly's Gulch native son, Lance Spearman, had been promoted to staff sergeant in the air force and was currently assigned at Elmendorf Air Force Base in Alaska.

Cliff swore under his breath.

Tasha looked over his shoulder at the newspaper. "What's wrong?"

"Winnie's got another bee up her you-know-what. The school board is going to vote next week on closing our school, and you can bet your last bottle of nail polish, Winnie's behind the move. She's never had any kids and doesn't have a clue how awful it'd be for our children to be bused clear to Brady."

"That's a long way?"

"For some of the ranch kids—like Jason someday—it'd be a two- or three-hour ride both ways, maybe worse during the winter. Plus, once our school is gone, Reilly's Gulch will die a slow, painful death. No one will want to move here, not if there's no local school."

He speared his fingers through his hair. "I'm going to have to be at that school board meeting next week."

"I'll watch Stevie. No problem."

He eyed her for a minute. "You know, I think we need to pack that auditorium with all the folks we can get, kids included. I'm going to make some calls. And next week, I'd like you to bring both of the children. I don't know about Winnie, but most of the school board members won't want to go against the community. If folks turn out in droves, no way will they vote to close our school.''

"If you really think my being here will help, of course I'll attend the meeting."

He held her gaze steadily. ''In a town this size, everybody counts.''

Turning back to her dinner preparations, Tasha drained the beans and poured them into a casserole dish, then stirred in a can of mushroom soup. Cliff's intense loyalty to Reilly's Gulch would make him a wonderful sheriff, but she couldn't help feeling her presence in his household would prove to be an embarrassment for him during his election campaign.

Yet she couldn't deny he needed her—or someone—to watch out for Stevie. And it was nice to know she counted for something.

Chapter Five

Every eye in the room was on her. Cliff didn't know how Tasha could handle that, strangers ogling her, but he supposed as a fashion model it came with the territory.

The school gymnasium was set up with folding chairs to seat more than a hundred people, the school board members on a riser up front. Holding Melissa's hand, Tasha glided down the center aisle, a pleasant smile on her face. She had to know all heads had turned her direction, that every whispering voice she heard was talking about her. That the men—married or not—were all speculating about her, fantasizing about her.

In a room full of ordinary people, most of them dressed in jeans and jackets, Tasha stood out like a Thoroughbred in a herd of cow ponies. The navy suit she wore was conservative but more appropriate to a New York business meeting than for a small-town school board session. Her stylish platform heels sent a far different message than the scruffy cowboy boots worn by most of the folks in the room. And her hair was pulled back in a sophisticated twist he doubted even Harriet at the beauty parlor could have managed.

An elementally masculine part of him felt a surge of pride that she was with him tonight. Something else told him they both might have been better off if she'd stayed at home. He shouldn't have exposed her to so much conjecture on the part of the good folks of Reilly's Gulch.

Tubby Sinclair elbowed him in the ribs and waggled his eyebrows suggestively. "Some housekeeper, Swain. Way to go!"

Cliff ignored him. "Come on, son," he said to Stevie. "Tasha has found us some seats."

A member of the King family, a man about forty, stopped him in the aisle. "Any luck finding a lead on the rustlers?"

"Not yet. Larry's checking with other jurisdictions. He'll keep you posted."

King didn't look pleased with Cliff's answer. And before Cliff could go another two steps an older couple who lived on the outskirts of town complained about teenagers racing cars on their road.

"I'll look into it," he told them.

Somebody else wanted to talk about the potholes in Main Street—which wouldn't be his responsibility even if he was elected sheriff—but he had to listen anyway.

Two people stopped him, wanting him to know Bobby Bruhn didn't have a chance of beating him come the June election; one other man, who hung out at Sal's, thought Bobby would be perfect for the sheriff's job because he wouldn't harass a guy for driving after having a couple of beers.

Cliff figured two out of three votes wasn't too bad.

The school board was about ready to start the meeting when he finally got to the chairs Tasha had saved for them.

"Sorry about that," he murmured, arranging Stevie between himself and Tasha. He held his hat on his lap.

"You seem to know just about everyone in town."

"Comes from growing up here."

"I feel like I'm overdressed for the occasion," she confided. "I should have realized...."

He gave her a reassuring smile. "You look great. Perfect, in fact."

The intimate, seductive smile she returned unnerved him, making him forget for an instant where he was and why. And that there were a hundred people watching them. His fingers closed around the brim of his Stetson, and he made sure the hat hid the sudden reaction of his body that had his jeans feeling several sizes too small.

Almost as soon as the opening ceremonies of the flag salute and benediction had been completed, Stevie started fidgeting in his chair. Melissa wasn't much better.

"This is boring, Mommy," she whispered.

"I know, honey." Tasha gave her daughter a one-arm squeeze and placed a kiss on top of the child's head. "But we want Stevie to be able to go to school close to home, don't we?"

Melissa shrugged. "I guess."

Tasha dug into her oversize shoulder bag for puzzle books and pencils to entertain the children. She'd expected them to get restless. She hadn't expected to feel so out of place herself.

She'd noticed Candy from the beauty shop in the crowd and the butcher from the grocery store. They'd both waved. Still, Tasha had felt ill at ease, like when the most popular girls in high school had shunned her. Tasha's mother had said it was because she was the prettiest girl on campus and they were jealous. Tasha had only known it hurt. She'd wanted to be their friend.

She wanted to be friends with these people of Reilly's Gulch, too, not simply feel as though she was on display. But then she forcefully reminded herself she wasn't planning to stay long in town.

The school district's business manager presented a grim financial picture for the next school year, numbers that mostly went over Tasha's head. Members of the school board commented, Winifred leading the pack anxious to close the school and save taxpayer dollars. Somehow Tasha suspected the only money the newspaper publisher was interested in saving was her own.

As the meeting droned on, she kept glancing at Cliff. Such a solid family man, he should be here with his wife and three or four stair-step children—not with an ersatz housekeeper who'd managed to scorch a second work shirt today. If Candy was

right—and Tasha didn't doubt it for a moment—
every woman in town had had her eye on Cliff since
he'd reached puberty. As much as he'd loved his
wife, he wasn't the kind of man who was meant to
remain single for long.

Idly stroking the back of Stevie's head as he bent
over a connect-the-dots puzzle, she envied the
woman who would land Cliff and be able to give
him more children. Drawing in a quick breath, she
fought the unexpectedly sharp stab of disappointment that she'd never be the one.

He glanced at her. "You okay?"

"Fine. Just a little tired of sitting, I suppose."

His lips twitched into a half smile. "They do like
to hear themselves talk, don't they?"

When members of the audience were finally allowed to speak, Chester O'Reilly was the first to
reach the microphone. Or maybe the townspeople
had planned it that way.

"I was in one of the first classes that attended
Reilly Elementary School in the 1920s. My children
and grandchildren graduated here, right in this very
room." Though age had given him a stoop to his
shoulders, nothing had diminished his powerful
voice or his passion, and his words reverberated
around the hushed audience.

"My great-grandchildren are going here now.
Everyone of 'em have skinned their knees on the
playground plenty of times and a few of 'em have
been switched for not behaving like they should.
And we all know—" with a flair for the dramatic,
he lowered his voice "—if we close our school, the

town will die. Nobody will move here, no new young families will want to settle here. They'll all go to Brady, or maybe Great Falls.

"And that means there won't be any need for a feed store or the diner. Harriet and her beauty shop might as well close the doors right now 'cause there won't be a soul who needs a haircut. Arnie might as well stop pumping gas at his garage. I can put my taxi service up on blocks. And there won't be anyone left to advertise in the *Register*," he said pointedly, eyeing Winifred, who ducked her head.

Turning away from the school board members, his gaze swept the room. "I say we find a way to keep our school." His voice boomed like a preacher determined to convert his flock.

Several members of the audience echoed his thought.

"Folks, I can't hear you!"

This time the response was louder. Someone started a chant: *"Keep our school! Keep our school!"*

Others joined in until practically the entire audience was standing, shouting and stomping their feet. Melissa and Stevie finally started to have a good time, joining in the chorus. Amused by the crowd's enthusiasm, Tasha got on her feet, too.

The school board chairman pounded his gavel. Nobody cared. They were having too much fun making their combined voices heard. Democracy at work, small-town style.

The chairman called for Deputy Swain to clear the room and help him restore order.

Cliff shrugged. "Sorry, it's my night off," he shouted over the noise of the crowd.

Everyone cheered except the duly elected school board members.

With a final bang of his gavel, the chairman ordered the topic tabled and the meeting adjourned.

The audience thought they had won the war. Tasha suspected the subject would be back on the table again at the next meeting, and would stay there until a solution to the school district's money problems could be found.

Cliff swooped Stevie up on his shoulders to get him out of the crush of people leaving the meeting hall. Tasha, with Melissa right in front of her, followed close behind them. Cliff and his broad shoulders made a perfect blocker to get them safely through the crowd.

Once outside, the cool evening air washed over Tasha and the crowd dispersed toward their cars. She drew a cleansing breath. Montana ought to bottle their air and sell it in New York City. An entrepreneur would make a real killing by framing a piece of the starlit sky, too, and hanging it over Manhattan.

"Hey, it's Unka Bry," Stevie cried from his perch on his father's shoulders.

The two Swain brothers shook hands and Tasha hugged her sister.

Melissa tugged on Bryant's arm. "Can you carry me on your shoulders like Uncle Cliff's doing for Stevie?"

"You sure you're not too big for that?" he asked with a teasing wink.

Melissa held up her arms. "I'll probably be too big next year. But now I'm *just* right."

Laughing, he hefted her in the air and Melissa squealed, linking her hands around his forehead.

Tasha smiled up at her daughter, then said to Ella, "Did you miss all the fun at the meeting?"

"Got here just in time for Chester's speech and the near riot," Ella said. "Jason was a little fussy and I was afraid to leave him alone with Rusty."

"What'd you do?"

"He called Sal and she came out to the ranch to baby-sit."

"Sal? Of Sal's Bar and Grill?"

Ella grinned. "Didn't you know? Rusty and Sal are quite an item. He stays in town every Saturday night, and I don't think it's because he's too drunk to drive home."

"Oh, my sakes!" Tasha giggled. "What a pair."

"Two of the nicest people I know."

Bryant had made a tour of the schoolyard with Melissa jiggling on his shoulders. As the crowd began to thin, he returned to where Tasha and Ella were standing and lowered Melissa to the ground. "Pony express package delivered, safe and sound," Bryant announced. "But this ol' man's shoulders may never be the same."

Ella gave him an affectionate slap on the arm. "We'll see just how tired you are when we get home."

"I trust that's a promise, Mrs. Swain."

Laughing, Ella's cheeks colored. "If you think you're up to it."

Melissa tugged on Tasha's sleeve. "Can we go home, Mommy. I'm really tired."

"I'm sorry, sweetie, and you were so good during the meeting." She hugged Ella again and thanked Bryant for entertaining her daughter. "I hope Jason's all right."

"Sal thinks he might be teething, but it seems so early."

"Didn't Mama tell you we Papadakis kids were the most advanced children in all of Queens? According to her, we were walking and talking and teething before she got us home from the hospital."

Ella laughed, but the shadow of a first-time mother's concerns hadn't quite vanished from her eyes as she walked off with her arm tucked in Bryant's.

With some effort, Tasha extricated Cliff from a conversation with a teenage boy. Then a younger child came up to throw his arms around Cliff for a hug. Cliff responded in a loving way, all the time bouncing his own son on his shoulders, and Tasha was struck again by what a natural father he was. No pretense, just an easy manner that youngsters of all ages understood.

"Looks like you're as popular with the younger set as you are with the local ladies," she teased as he held open the truck door for Stevie and Melissa to climb into the jump seat behind the front seat.

"Hey, I'd adopt them all if I could," he said,

laughing. "The kids, that is. But their parents might object."

"There're probably some days when their parents would be happy to take you up on your offer."

"Yeah, you're probably right." He grinned, taking her elbow to steady her as she climbed into the passenger seat. She really shouldn't have worn her platform heels tonight. Usually she had a better sense of style, but in Reilly's Gulch the rules had changed.

She waited as he went around to the driver's side and got in beside her, noticing how he checked to make sure the kids had their seat belts on. An attentive father like Cliff really ought to have a house full of children. Swallowing hard, she faced again the truth that children weren't something she'd ever be able to give a man.

"So, what'd you think of the meeting?" he asked as he twisted the key in the ignition.

"No one was keeping it a secret about how they felt."

He chuckled. "That's true enough. But I suppose that's the same in a big city."

"I suppose, except..."

Waiting for another pickup to back out of its spot, he glanced in her direction. "Except what?"

"I don't know." And she wasn't too sure how honest she ought to be with him about her uncomfortable feelings. "There's an expression in New York—shoulder candy."

His eyebrows shot up. "Shoulder candy?"

"Sometimes men, usually wealthy playboys, want

to be seen with an attractive woman on their arm, so they date models. Basically the men think of the women as objects to be shown off, not real people.'' She folded her hands in her lap, embarrassed that she'd mentioned the subject. She shouldn't have.

''Is that why you think I invited you to the meeting?''

''No, not really. It's just that...'' Both of the children in the back seat had curled up, already close to being asleep. Even so, she kept her voice so low only Cliff could hear her. ''That happened to me a couple of times after my divorce. It's humiliating, being nothing more than a plastic statue, hardly even expected to speak unless spoken to. I quit dating after that until I started seeing Nick socially.'' Only later did she realize he'd wanted her tied to him because of the financial benefits he gained, not because he cared about her personally.

Pulling over to the side of the road, Cliff stopped the truck and left the engine running. He covered her folded hands with his. His fingers were long, his nails neatly trimmed, the palm of his hand warm and slightly rough with calluses. Not like those playboys in New York or the stockbrokers who thrived on adrenaline highs from watching themselves and others make or lose fortunes within minutes. No, not like them at all. Stronger. Steadier. More connected to the things that mattered in life.

''I won't say I wasn't proud to be seen with you tonight. I was. Any man would be. But that's not why I wanted you to come to the school with me. And that's *not* how I feel about you.''

A frisson of sweet pleasure rippled through her. "Thank you." He squeezed her hands. "And next time, if you want to talk, you go right ahead. But you'll probably have to wrestle the mike away from Chester to do it."

She laughed, and ran her thumb over the top of Cliff's hand, rubbing lightly. "Oh, I think I can handle Chester. He's nothing but a pussycat."

"I won't tell him you said so." His lips twitched ever so slightly. "Ol' Chester thinks he's one tough hombre and a lady killer to boot."

"We city girls aren't easily intimidated."

As Cliff pulled the truck back onto the roadway, Tasha wondered if she could handle her growing feelings for the man who was her temporary employer as easily as she could a ninety-year-old man with visions of expanding his taxi service in Reilly's Gulch.

TWO DAYS LATER, Cliff got a letter in the mail. It was his day off and he'd gone over to the main ranch early to help Bryant and Rusty install a new water pump in the well.

Scanning the letter quickly, he cursed, then marched outside where Tasha and the kids were puttering in the flower beds, planting snapdragons and pansies she'd bought at the feed store. He waved the letter in the air.

"Will you look at this!" he complained.

Tasha glanced up from her work, a streak of dirt on her right cheek. "What is it?"

"What's wrong, Uncle Cliff?"

Stevie grunted something, but he was busy with a full-size hoe trying to chop weeds that had grown up in the walkway. He didn't appear too interested in Cliff's problems.

Cliff passed the letter to Tasha. "Bobby Bruhn is complaining about every single problem in the whole county and blaming it on Sheriff Colman and, by extension, me."

She read over the letter. "Rustlers on the loose, kids disrupting neighborhoods, high-speed car chases, potholes—" She glanced up. "Is the sheriff responsible for—"

"No, of course not. Bobby's just trying to lay everything wrong in the county on Colman's shoulders." And his own.

With a sigh, she sat back on her haunches. "One thing Bobby can't blame on the sheriff is the accusation that you're living with a woman you aren't married to."

"What? Let me see that." He snatched the letter back from her, reading the final paragraph he'd missed. It reeked of innuendo, of Winnie's morality policing at work. "I swear, if I ever get my hands on Bobby or his—" He clamped his mouth shut before he completed the threat. It would be just his luck Bobby would get killed in a barroom brawl and Winifred would decide to blame Cliff. As Tasha looked at him, the question of her leaving obvious in her eyes, Cliff was struck by how *right* she looked sitting there. Working in his garden, playing with his kid. Doing things a *wife* would do. Before she could ask the question that was obviously on her mind, he said, "You know what this means?"

Her eyes slowly blinked closed. "Yes, we should have left—"

"No." He squatted down beside her, and with his fingertip he wiped away the dirt smudge on her cheek. "It means I've got to run a full-fledged campaign, including sending out letters to every voter in the whole damn county. I've gotta write 'em and get 'em printed. Stuff 'em. Lick 'em. How am I gonna do all that if I don't have a campaign manager to help me?"

She stared at him blankly. "Campaign manager?"

Stevie was still hacking away at the weeds, with decreasing success and enthusiasm. Melissa, distracted by a roly-poly bug, had lost interest in the snapdragons she'd been sticking in the ground.

"Don't tell me you're going to hold out on me till I double your salary. That's highway robbery. An extra hundred a month. That's all I can afford."

"B-but—" she stammered, bewildered.

He got up and pulled her to her feet. Her hands were so delicate, the bones as fragile as a bird's, they practically vanished in his. He had a quick flash of those same hands caressing him intimately, and he had to catch his breath before he could speak.

"I'm no good with words, not the way I know you must be. I need you to write the letter, something about people being able to feel safe in the county because they have someone experienced in charge. Someone who cares."

"What makes you think I could write—"

"Because every night I see you curled up at the end of the couch reading a book. And you got more books piled all over the table in the bedroom."

A flush colored her cheeks. "They're romance novels. Not exactly texts on political science."

"What do you think I read on the few occasions I get around to reading? Stuff on the law. Or collecting DNA samples. Tracking missing persons. Not the kind of prose a voter would find motivating."

"I don't know, Cliff. This election is so important to you. I've never been considered all that smart—"

"It's damned important. That's why I need you." Taking her by the hand, he walked her to the porch and sat her down on the steps. A light breeze was blowing from the west, and a few clouds were building over the mountains threatening an early summer thunderstorm. He sat down next to her. "My brother and I were abandoned by our birth mother when we were about four years old."

Tasha gasped and her eyes widened but she didn't say anything, so he went on, for the moment trying not to think about how soft her cheek had felt when he'd touched her.

"The Swain family adopted us and brought us to the ranch. They were terrific parents, and both Bry and I owe a lot to them, but the abandonment affected us in different ways. Bry set his roots down deep in the land, particularly in the Double S. To some extent I feel the same way. But..." He leaned forward, clasping his hands together, trying not to let his earliest memories hurt too much. "I always had the feeling our mother couldn't have *wanted* to give us up. For some reason she was *forced* into it, like she was too poor to keep us or something. So I became a cop, not so much because I wanted to catch bad guys, but because if somebody needed a little help, I wanted to be the one who saw to it they got what they needed. I can remember her crying...." He turned his head toward Tasha. "Does that sound crazy?" Tasha placed her hand on his back, feeling the flex of his muscles beneath her palm, the heat of his skin burning through his work shirt. Her chest tightened with emotion. How could any woman give up her babies unless she was forced to by dire circumstances? "No, it doesn't sound crazy."

"You could write stuff like that without making it sound—I don't know—sappy. I couldn't do it myself."

The press of tears made her blink; the unwarranted pride she felt in his glowing idealism, as though she were a part of his spirit, made her heart ache.

"I think you could do anything you wanted to do, Cliff, but I'd be honored to try to write the letter for you. I'll lick envelopes and put stamps on as many as it takes for you to win the election. And you don't have to pay me a dime extra."

His eyes met hers, the passion for his cause obvious. She felt a bolt of electricity as powerful as lightning arcing across the sky. Imperceptibly, she felt herself leaning forward, wanting him to—

"Dad, can I quit now?" Stevie whined.

"Sure," Cliff said distractedly, his gaze not straying from Tasha's face. "You did good, bucko."

"Now can I ride Star Song?" Stevie asked. "Aunt Tasha wouldn't let me, not without you around."

"Me, too. Me, too," Melissa pleaded.

The kids were on their feet, hopping around, effectively breaking the mood. Tasha tried to tell herself the disruption was for the best. But her foolish heart wasn't in it, wanting instead to have Cliff hold her and kiss her.

Cliff stood, too. "Tell you what. In lieu of extra salary, how 'bout I give you that riding lesson I promised you?"

"No, I couldn't—"

"Peaches will be so gentle, you'll love her. And I won't leave your side. I promise."

"But I've got these flowers—"

"They'll wait."

He tugged her to her feet again. She wanted to go with him wherever he wanted to take her—even if it was to her certain death beneath the hooves of an enraged horse, she thought grimly.

Without releasing her hand, he led her around the house to the corral. Stevie and Melissa raced ahead of them.

"I get to go first!" Stevie shouted. "It's my horse."

"Ladies first," Cliff reminded his son.

"I volunteer to go last," Tasha said. A knot was

forming in her stomach and her mouth was already as dry as if she'd been chewing tumbleweeds.

His wickedly teasing chuckle didn't contain a bit of sympathy for her. She was, she realized, going to have to get past her fear of horses—at least for the next few weeks. Once back in New York, it would be easy to avoid contact with the beasts.

Once back in New York, she'd never see Cliff again. The knot in her stomach tightened and this time it wasn't for fear of horses.

She lingered outside the corral while the horses were saddled, amazed at the way Stevie used a step-ladder to give him enough height to heft the saddle onto Star Song's back. Definitely a young cowboy in the making and a determined one. Melissa was equally eager. More than once Tasha had to swallow a warning cry when she got too close to the horse's hooves.

"If we all want to ride together, I'm going to have to bring back some more horses from the main ranch," Cliff said.

"Don't bother on my account." She sugarcoated her response with mock sweetness.

"Of course, I could always saddle up Henry for you."

Her eyes widened. "The mule?" she gasped. "You wouldn't!"

His laughter whipped across the corral like a blowing leaf, making Peaches sidestep away from Cliff. Despite her fears, Tasha experienced a giddy sensation, his teasing ways causing her to feel light-headed.

Maybe it was just the fresh air, the wide-open spaces that had her on edge. She wasn't used to being able to see halfway into tomorrow. In New York, the horizon was the next skyscraper unless you were higher than the twenty-fifth floor. Here the miles stretched out in every direction and her eyes seemed to have developed a pleasant ache from exercising muscles for long-distance vision.

"Okay, your turn, Ms. Goldilocks."

Her attention snapped back to Cliff. The children were already mounted together on Star Song's back and Cliff was holding Peaches's reins in his hand. The mare had soulful brown eyes and long, curling lashes. She looked harmless. But Tasha suspected appearances could be deceiving when it came to a creature that weighed eight hundred pounds.

"What are they going to say in New York when you get back to town and admit you went all the way to Montana and never even got on a horse?"

"That I'm a darn smart city girl."

"Come on," he cajoled. "You don't want Melissa to think you're chicken, do you?"

Tasha wouldn't mind about her daughter, but at some deeper level she didn't want to disappoint Cliff. Obviously he was used to women who were comfortable around horses. She should at least try....

Getting over the fence was easy. Figuring how to get herself into the saddle was a different matter.

"Maybe I should wait until you find me one of those miniature horses," she suggested. "One about three feet tall."

He held out his hands, cupping them. "Put your left foot in my hands and grab a handful of mane. I'll boost you up. Swing your other leg over the saddle just like the cowboys do in the movies. Nothing to it."

He made it sound so easy. It might have been, too, if her legs hadn't started to tremble and the damn horse hadn't moved just as she got halfway between the ground and the saddle.

She screamed and hooked her arm around the saddle horn, her right leg pinwheeling in the air. Cliff got his hand under her butt and shoved. She grunted. So did he, or it might have been a swallowed laugh she heard. The horse snorted.

Finally righting herself, her legs splayed in what felt like a split, she grabbed the saddle horn with both hands. Until now she'd never been afraid of heights. Skyscrapers were her second home. Suddenly from the top of a horse, the ground looked a long way away.

Then, to compound her problems, the horse took a step without being invited to, and Tasha's heart galloped.

"Definitely not the most graceful mount I've ever seen," Cliff muttered. His hand was warm on her thigh, branding her through her designer jeans.

"You ought to see me getting on a subway. Sheer beauty in motion."

"I never thought otherwise." He looked up at her with more than amusement in his blue eyes, something hot and needy, and Tasha felt an echo of the same feeling low in her body.

"Isn't this fun, Mommy?" Melissa cried.

"I think it could be dangerous." She thought only of Cliff and his potent masculinity, her whispered voice sounding breathless, husky to her own ears. "Very dangerous."

Chapter Six

Early the next morning, Tasha called New York. Writing a campaign letter for Cliff and stuffing a few envelopes was one thing, but she couldn't let herself get too involved with him and his son. Or with the town of Reilly's Gulch. She didn't belong here. That much was obvious and had been since she arrived. Now was the time to pull herself together and begin reestablishing her career.

Nick Mecouri was history.

Peter Strauss was an even bigger agent, and he had once courted Tasha professionally, trying to get her to sign with his agency. No time like the present, she thought as she waited for him to pick up the phone. Cliff was already outside working with the horses. The children had tagged along after him as if he were the Pied Piper, giving her a few minutes to herself.

"Tasha, my love." Peter greeted her with his usual booming voice. She could almost smell the cigar he perpetually smoked. "It's so good to hear from you."

''You, too, Peter. How's New York?'' Leaning against the kitchen counter, she glanced outside at the mountains on the distant horizon, a truly beautiful sight as the morning sun changed them from gray to rose.

''Spring is in the air, which means fall fashions are everywhere you look. It's going to be a lovely season. Smashing new designs. Skirts are up. Definitely up.''

''Fortunately my legs are one of my best features.'' No harm in a little self-promotion, although, in truth, her hair had always been the thing most people noticed first.

''They are indeed, lovey. You'll wow them, I'm sure.''

''I hope so, which is why I called.'' She twirled the phone cord around her finger, noticing she'd broken a nail and the polish was chipped. That wasn't like her at all to ignore any detail of her appearance. ''You've heard Nick is no longer representing me?''

There was a long pause, the silence on the line ominous. ''Yes, lovey, I've heard.''

''That means I'm looking for a new agent. The first person I thought of was you, Peter. I think we'd do well together. I regret now I didn't sign with you years ago.'' Though she had to admit Nick had done a good job getting her plum assignments. It was in the personal relationship where he'd failed her. Or maybe in some way, she'd failed him.

''You flatter me, my dear.'' He was hedging. She could hear it in his voice, his hesitation. ''The fact is, the agency is working with a large number of clients at the moment. As much as I'd, ah, like to represent you, I'm not sure I could do you justice. You know how it is, my dear.''

"No, I don't, Peter. Two years ago you were dying to have me sign with you. I'm a top model and draw the big bucks. Surely things haven't changed—"

"Two years is a long time in this business. You know that. And lately there've been rumors. Not that I believe them, you understand," he hastened to add.

Frowning, Tasha sat down heavily on a kitchen chair, the phone cord stretching halfway across the room. "What rumors?"

"Oh, something about a nervous breakdown. Not unusual in our—"

"Nervous breakdown? Who on earth would say a thing like that?"

"Well, my dear, you did leave town in a bit of a hurry. Nick said he tried to reach you for a Renaldi showing and had no luck. He did find another lovely girl. Let me see, her name was..."

Tasha stopped listening. It wasn't enough that Nick had two-timed her with a girl so young she ought to still be modeling diapers. Now he was spreading rumors that could effectively kill her career.

Her hand closed tightly around the phone, squeezing until her knuckles went white. The rotten, no-good, two-timing—

Managing to save her dignity, she concluded her conversation with Peter as quickly as possible and hung up. There were other agents in New York.

Nick's effort to undercut her career couldn't have reached the ears of all of them.

She was still sitting at the kitchen table contemplating her next call when Cliff came in the house. She marveled at the way he moved, sauntering in a loose-limbed way that was both relaxed and extremely masculine, just this side of an arrogant swagger.

He tossed his hat on the table, troubled by the frown that tugged at Tasha's forehead. "Looks like you either lost your best friend or scorched another one of my shirts," he teased. "Which is it?"

Her forced smile didn't reach her sky-blue eyes. "My former fiancé is trying to put the kibosh on my career. How's that for great news first thing in the morning?"

Something twisted in Cliff's gut. "You talked to him this morning?"

"No, I called another agent, one who *used* to want to represent me. Now—because I've had a nervous breakdown, according to Nick—he won't touch me." She pressed her fingertips to her temple as though trying to rub away a headache. "Sweet guy, huh?"

Impulsively, he stepped behind Tasha's chair and began to massage her neck, trying to ease her tension. Her collarless blouse dipped an inch or two both in front and back, baring her skin to his touch. Her flesh looked as creamy as fresh milk, her bones delicate. In contrast, his hands appeared big and clumsy on her.

"So, what are you going to do?" he asked.

"Call more agents, I guess." With a soft moan of pleasure, she let her head fall forward. "You've got talented hands."

"They're rough. Not what you're used to." Not those of an agent who'd let her down, maybe somebody she still cared about despite her denials.

"They feel fine to me. Strong. Gentle. If you ever decide to give up playing cops and robbers, you could go into the massage business."

"There's probably not a real big demand for that here in Reilly's Gulch."

"Hmm. I'd sign up and you can bet so would every woman in town."

"That a fact?" As much as he was enjoying the moment, he had to keep reminding himself that Tasha had called New York because she intended to return there. She had a career and probably made damn good money when her agent wasn't ripping her off. Montana wasn't her thing.

Sighing again, she shifted her shoulders. "You could always move to New York. You'd make millions there."

"Having millions has never been particularly important to me and living in a big city doesn't hold a great deal of appeal, either." He'd lived in L.A. for a year—where he'd first met Ella—but beyond the extra police training he'd received while assigned to the LAPD, the only redeeming value had been living near the beach. Stevie had loved that part.

"No, I don't suppose you'd like New York."

"But you do." He couldn't believe otherwise.

"Manhattan is—" she hesitated while he ran his thumbs down along the sides of her spine, groaning slightly "—exciting."

By being so pliable beneath his hands, she was arousing him. His erection pressed painfully against the fly of his jeans, his blood pulsing hot and hard. He wanted to turn her around, draw her to her feet, massage other, even more interesting parts of her elegant body. Kiss her everywhere. Undo the clip that held her hair back and bury his face in the provocative scent of her shampoo. And then he wanted to carry her into the bedroom, make love to her until they were both sated, forgetting that she'd be leaving soon.

Dumb plan. A man shouldn't get used to things he couldn't keep.

As though he'd been burned, he pulled his hands away from the sweet, sensual feel of Tasha's back.

Turning, she lifted her head, her eyes heavy-lidded and nearly black with her own arousal, her lips slightly parted as though waiting for his kiss.

"Is something wrong?" she questioned in a sultry voice.

"No, I..." He snatched up his hat from the table. "I just came in to tell you the kids and I are going for a ride over to Salters Creek to catch some tadpoles."

Alarm flared in her eyes. "On horseback?"

"Melissa's on Peaches. She'll be fine, I promise, and we'll be back in time for lunch."

She glanced at the clock on the stove. "I don't know..."

"Of course, if you'd like to come along—"

"No, thanks. I'll keep my feet on terra firma, if you don't mind. It's just that I worry—"

Unable to resist, he skimmed the back of his hand on her cheek. "Melissa's doing fine with her riding lessons. Honestly. Nothing bad will happen to her."

"I know." Drawing in a deep breath, then expelling it, she nodded. "Just don't let her do anything foolish."

"I won't." Cliff was the one tempted to do something foolish, and he planned to fight the urge as hard as he could. "We'll be back in a couple of hours."

"I'll start drafting your campaign letter after I make a couple more phone calls."

He swallowed the raw pain of reality. "Great. See you later."

WITHIN THE NEXT few days, Tasha turned Cliff's dining room into campaign headquarters, and she was enjoying herself. She'd gotten voter registration lists from the county recorder and had arranged to have stationery printed at a shop in Great Falls. Unlike Bobby Bruhn, whose campaign literature had been printed by the *Reed County Register,* Cliff had to pay for his materials himself. The first letter to be mailed would include a request for contributions.

Ella sat across from Tasha at the dining table where they were stuffing envelopes. It was nice to have company when Cliff was at work. The evenings, Tasha found, could get lonely with only a book to read and an operatic CD for companionship.

Strange, she'd never felt that way in New York, relieved to have the quiet of her own apartment after a busy day of work. Here she *missed* Cliff even if he was only as far away as the barn.

"So, how're you getting along with Cliff?" Ella asked, carefully folding a letter and slipping it into an envelope.

Tasha's hands stilled. Her sister had arrived after dinner, enjoyed the children for an hour or two and stayed to help with the mailing. Melissa and Stevie had lost interest in the project early on and had since gone to bed.

Only now had Ella mentioned the one subject Tasha would just as soon avoid. "Fine," she said lightly. "I haven't scorched one of his shirts in days." Of course, she hadn't ironed, either. In fact, she'd dropped off his dirty shirts at a one-hour laundry when she'd been in Great Falls. Well worth the trip, she thought, admiring her cleverness.

Ella adjusted her glasses more comfortably on her nose. "You mean to tell me you've been living with Cliff for what, two weeks, and the best you've done is not burn his shirts?"

Intentionally misunderstanding the question, Tasha said, "You didn't really expect me to turn into a gourmet chef, did you? I did get the grocery store to carry some ready-made pasta salads, and that's helped, but I'm never going to be Martha Stewart in the kitchen."

"But I thought—" Ella's expression clouded over.

"Surely when you suggested I help Cliff out by

being a nanny you weren't playing matchmaker, sister dear?'' Tasha asked with mock surprise.

''Well, no, not exactly.'' She snatched up the next letter and folded it crookedly. ''Well, maybe a little. I mean, Cliff's a pretty terrific guy and I thought maybe...''

''Uh-huh. And you didn't notice the long commute from here to New York—or Paris, for that matter—where all those lucrative modeling jobs happen.'' Not that she'd had any recent job offers in either place. But it was only a matter of time. She'd contacted several more agents. They were considering her portfolio.

''Well, there's no harm in wanting my sister living close to me, is there?''

''No, of course not. And I feel the same way. But given my life-style, I'd say we're going to have to settle for a few weeks' vacation a year to get together. Maybe you can even come to New York in the fall and we'll do some shopping. You used to love that.''

Ella glanced at Jason, who was sleeping peacefully in his portable playpen in the corner of the room. ''Funny, the thought of leaving Montana even on a vacation doesn't hold a whole lot of appeal. I've even convinced the folks to come out this summer to visit.''

''Dad, too?''

''I've promised him his own personal cab driver.''

Tasha choked on a laugh. ''Not Chester?''

''The two of them will get along famously, I'm

sure. Besides, I thought maybe—if things worked out between you and Cliff—they'd be coming out here for another wedding. I caught a glimpse of Cliff looking at you at the school board meeting and I don't think he's worried about how well you can iron his shirts. That's why I thought…''

Scorching heat flooded Tasha's cheeks. ''It's not like that. I mean, he might find me attractive but he knows…'' She tidied the stack of stuffed envelopes and shoved them aside. There were a dozen reasons why it didn't make sense for her and Cliff to become involved, even for a brief affair. And there was one reason in particular why he'd never choose her for a wife, a reason she'd never told her family and didn't intend to blab now. ''I don't belong in Montana, Ella. You know that. I'm terrified of horses and heaven forbid I'd ever meet a rattlesnake or a mountain lion. And in case you hadn't noticed, there aren't a whole lot of modeling jobs here in Reilly's Gulch.''

''But you wouldn't have to—''

''As you say, Cliff's a really nice guy and a great brother-in-law to you. But friendship is all he and I will ever have together. Let's let it go at that, okay?''

The suspicious look in Ella's eyes suggested she didn't think the topic was entirely closed but she was gracious enough to change the subject.

Tucking a strand of flyaway hair behind her ear, Tasha had the feeling she'd only gained a temporary reprieve from her sister's matchmaking. Ella could be very determined when she set her mind on something, no doubt a characteristic of being so damn intelligent. But there wasn't anything that would change the fact that Tasha would never be able to give Cliff what she suspected he wanted most of all. And it wasn't someone who could iron his shirts.

OVER THE COURSE of the next few days, Cliff decided in order to run for an elective office and maintain any sort of a normal life, he needed to be at least two people. Three would have been better.

In addition to caring for his own animals, he spent what time he could with Stevie and had been giving Melissa and Tasha riding lessons, though clearly Tasha remained anxious any time she got near a horse.

Meanwhile, when he wasn't working, he'd met with the Reed County Merchants Association about shoplifting problems. Chester O'Reilly had dragged him to a meeting of some folks who wanted to set up a tourist information office. And he'd had to give two campaign speeches, both of them at senior citizen homes where half the audience had dozed off in the middle of Bobby Bruhn's incredibly boring speech, Cliff recalled with a grin. Fortunately Tasha had given him some tips to perk up his talk which had kept the seniors not only awake but asking questions.

Thank God for Tasha, he thought as he wheeled into the drive at his house. Without her baby-sitting Stevie he never would have been able to run for office.

And damn it all, he wanted to be sheriff! Just

yesterday he'd gotten a call about an abandoned baby at a bus stop in Brady. He'd found the mother not two blocks away. The poor kid—only sixteen years old—had been so distraught, she hadn't known what to do or how to care for her baby. On his own, Cliff had driven her to a homeless shelter in Great Falls. With a little luck—and some help— he figured mother and child would be okay.

He parked the truck and climbed out. Despite his fatigue, his footsteps were light in anticipation of seeing Tasha—and the kids, he quickly amended. More and more he'd begun looking forward to coming home. And at last he had a night off.

Entering through the back door, he hung his hat on a peg and walked through the silent kitchen, making his way toward the living room.

Since Tasha had moved in, he'd grown used to hearing classical music coming from the CD player.

He wasn't used to seeing his son twirling around in the middle of the room in his socks, strutting on his toes, and brandishing a broken broom handle in the air. Meanwhile, Melissa, who was wearing a makeshift skirt made out of pink net, gyrated around Stevie like a colorful butterfly with a broken wing. Tasha, an audience of one, sat on the couch beaming her approval.

Cliff paused at the doorway and leaned against the doorjamb taking in the scene, not sure whether to laugh or call for the men in the white coats.

The music ended and Tasha applauded enthusiastically. "That was wonderful! You're a truly talented ballet troop! Lincoln Center, here we come!"

Shoving away from the doorway, Cliff said, "Funny, I thought they'd both gotten mad cow disease."

Both children squealed when they saw him and came running, throwing their arms around his waist. His throat tightened, suddenly realizing he'd miss Melissa almost as much as Tasha when they left.

"Did you see me, Daddy?"

"We went to a *ballet*, Uncle Cliff. Don't I look pretty?"

"I'm the hero," Stevie informed him. "He slays dragons 'n stuff and Melissa's Sleeping Beauty. I woke her up."

"I can see that." Hunkering down to their level, he hugged them back. Over the top of their heads, his gaze met Tasha's. Her eyes glittered with amusement, her half smile not at all innocent. "A ballet?"

"I mentioned the other day that I wanted to take them to a children's matinee," she said. "In Great Falls."

Cliff vaguely recalled the conversation. Lately he'd been distracted, and it wasn't entirely because of the election campaign. "I thought you meant a movie. Like a cartoon or something."

She lifted her shoulders in a nonchalant shrug. "You can get cartoons on TV. I noticed an advertisement when I was arranging for your campaign literature and I wanted them to experience a little culture."

He was trying to decide if he should take offense at her comment when Stevie tugged on his shirt to get his attention.

"In the middle of the show, during inner-mission, I got to go up on stage, Daddy. I blew on a horn and I did real good."

A ridiculous sense of pride swept through Cliff. Rationally he knew his nearly six-year-old son couldn't have been that great on any musical instrument. Yet he was inordinately pleased with his son's success. Maybe when Stevie was older he'd arrange for some music lessons. His son might not want to be a rancher or a cop, and Cliff wanted him to have all the options he could.

He gave the boy another hug. "Good for you, bucko."

"I got to play the tambourine," Melissa announced.

"Is that so?" he asked. "And I bet you were terrific."

"Of course." She flipped her long blond hair behind her shoulder. "But I'd rather be a ballerina than a musician. They're prettier."

"Hey, I thought you wanted to be a cowgirl," Cliff teased.

A little panicky that the two careers weren't compatible, Melissa glanced to her mother for help. "Can't I be both?"

Tasha unfolded herself from the couch, coming to her feet as gracefully as any dancer would. "Not too many cows at Lincoln Center, honey. But you have a few years yet before you have to decide which you'd like to be."

Assuring them dinner would be ready in a few minutes, Tasha strolled into the kitchen using the sexy walk that put significant parts of his anatomy on edge. Cliff was assigned the role of audience-of-one while she got things on the table.

That was fine by him, except his mind kept measuring the sweet sway of her hips and the seductive length of her legs below the short skirt she wore. He clenched his teeth, wondering if there would be time for a cold shower before dinner...or if it would do any good.

AFTER BATHS and bedtime stories, Cliff and Tasha tucked the children in for the night. Working the evening shift, he often missed being home when Stevie went to bed. And now, with the four of them, it felt oddly right. Familiar and satisfying.

Back in the living room after the children were well on their way to dreamland, Cliff rooted around in his collection of CDs. Like a lot of evenings lately, Tasha was elbow-deep at the cluttered dining table sorting responses to his campaign letter, many of them containing a small check or a few dollars in cash. In neat, small handwriting, she recorded each contribution in a ledger, determined that his campaign financial reports would be accurate.

She glanced up when the music started, her eyebrows raised in question.

"I figure if you can introduce my boy to ballet, it's only fittin' I teach you the finer points of Texas two-stepping."

She laughed softly and shook her head. "No, I don't think so."

"Hey, it can't be as scary as riding a horse, can it? Even with me doing the leading?"

"I still have a lot of work to do. Remember, I took the day off—"

He slipped the pen from her hand, placing it on the table. Her eyes slightly wary and as blue as a meadow flower on a spring morning, she stood at his urging. She'd changed clothes after dinner. Barefoot, she was now wearing jeans and a light sweater, a fabric so soft it begged for a man's caress. The music in the background pulsated at a fast beat but no quicker than his heart.

"Word has it your employer's a generous guy," he said, leading her into the living room where there was room to move around. "He'd probably give you the whole day off, if you asked. Evenings, too."

"I wouldn't want to take advantage of him."

Relishing the chance to touch her, he positioned them in front of the CD player. "What you ought to be worrying about is me stepping on your toes."

Tasha drew an unsteady breath, worried about something far different than her toes. The heat of his hand felt too good where he'd placed it, his thumb just brushing below the swell of her breast. The scent of the spray starch she'd used on his shirt mixed with his spicy aftershave, combining in a masculine bouquet that was uniquely his own. Despite her best efforts to prevent it, need coiled through her midsection and she ached for the sweet promise of his body and hers, together.

"Now do what I do," he directed. "It's pretty much like walking except you're going backward."

He held her as though they were about to waltz. "Here we go—slow, slow, quick, quick, slow. That's the way."

She felt clumsy, graceless, unable to concentrate on a few simple movements, focused instead on the man who held her so lightly. His hand had slid to the small of her back, his forearm now brushing the side of her breast, his left palm cradling her right hand.

"I've never done this before," she told him, more breathless than she should have been.

"It's okay. You'll catch on in a minute." His voice was husky, too, and persuasive.

Her feet tangled and a nervous giggle escaped as she added a slow instead of a quick-quick step. He caught her, his arm solid and supporting around her. As tall as she was, she often felt like a giant dancing with a man. Cliff made her feel almost petite. Vulnerable. And distinctly feminine.

One song ended and the next began at a slower pace, the lyrics proclaiming devotion to a love that could never be. Cliff's hand closed more firmly around her ribs as the mood changed and he drew her closer. Her feet came to a halt, the warm torment of his nearness impeding both thought and movement.

She looked into his eyes and the air escaped her lungs at the stark need she saw reflected there. With only a heartbeat of hesitation, he covered her mouth with his. The sensation shattered her with delight.

His lips were firm and warm, perfectly shaped to mold with hers. He took control of the kiss when the single pass of his tongue across her lips had her opening for him. He tasted of black coffee and potent masculinity. She responded eagerly, hungering for what had been so temptingly near and yet so unattainable.

Her breasts pressed against his broad chest and she felt his robust arousal at the apex of her thighs. Every nerve ending in her body responded. She wanted this. She wanted Cliff. And with what small modicum of reason still remained, she knew she wasn't being smart.

Too soon she'd leave; too soon she'd go back to the life that was hers.

Pressing her hands to his chest, she broke the kiss. Her breath came in quick pants. So did his. Her instincts complained bitterly that she hadn't allowed the moment to reach its ultimate conclusion. Here in the living room, if need be. Or mere steps down the hall in a bedroom—his or hers.

Forcefully she reminded herself why she'd come to Montana, that she hadn't been looking for a relationship, even a temporary one. She'd sworn off men.

Regaining her breath and a small part of her equilibrium, she said, "You do a heck of a two-step, Deputy Swain."

He framed her face with his big hands. "So do you, Goldilocks."

"I think we'd be better off to stick with ballet."

His eyes were so dark with arousal, there was barely a rim of blue around the irises. "I suppose

I'd better defer to the wisdom of my campaign manager. For now.''

His last words posed both promise and threat. Tasha wasn't at all sure what she should hope for, and was afraid to consider the implications of her weakening resolve.

Chapter Seven

A picket line snaked its way in front of the school gymnasium, parents and children alike waving Save Our School signs and shouting the same slogan. From the looks of the crowd, Tasha concluded there were even more people in attendance at this school board meeting than had come to last week's.

Melissa's sign clipped Tasha's shoulder. "Easy, honey. You don't want to poke someone in the eye."

"I got bumped."

"I know." She took her daughter's hand firmly in hers. "You just have to be careful."

Walking four abreast with Cliff and his son, Tasha self-consciously realized she was a fraud. They might look like a family, but they weren't. She wasn't even an official resident of Reilly's Gulch. Certainly not a registered voter.

Ever since the night Cliff had kissed her, the electricity between them had arced to a higher voltage. She'd been afraid even his casual touch would set off a power surge that would dim her good reason; she'd been afraid to get too close.

And she'd had the feeling he was circling her, watching, waiting for another opportunity, that the next time neither of them would be able to stop their reactions from accelerating out of control.

The chanting grew louder as a black town car pulled up to the curb and a tall, distinguished gentleman got out.

"Who's that?" Tasha asked Cliff over the noise of the crowd.

"State Superintendent of Schools Marc Toomey from Helena. He's the one who's actually going to shut us down."

No wonder the picketers had become so agitated; they barely opened a path wide enough for the man to walk into the building. Immediately the crowd poured in after him, funneling through the double doorway. She spotted Sal and Rusty holding hands as they shoved their way inside. Candy McCloud had a young boy in tow; she turned and waved in Cliff's direction, nearly losing her grip on her son.

Tasha quickly suppressed an unwarranted burst of jealousy. She had no more right to feel possessive about Cliff than she did to voice an opinion about the future of Reilly's Gulch and its educational facilities.

By the time the school board chairman finally gaveled the crowd to order, every chair was filled and there was standing room only at the back of the gym. The first thing the chairman did was turn the meeting over to Marc Toomey. He rose from his chair in the front row and took the microphone. His gray hair was neatly styled, his suit impeccably designed.

With few preliminaries, he got right to the heart of the matter. ''I understand how much you all want to keep your school open, but unless there's a substantial infusion of money into the district, Reilly's Gulch Elementary School will have to close.''

There were boos and hisses from the audience.

Walking in front of the risers, mike in hand, he was an imposing, authoritative figure. ''There's no way the district can pay its bills for the next school year and it's against the law to operate on a deficit budget.''

''Congress does it all the time,'' a man complained from the back of the room.

He shook his head. ''The federal government also prints its own money. The Reilly's Gulch School District can't do that.''

''We could raise our own taxes,'' someone suggested.

''That, I'm afraid, would take more than a year to approve and implement. Your school still couldn't open in September. It's not that I am unsympathetic to your concerns. It's simply that without an infusion of close to fifty thousand dollars, the school can't operate. Although we're certainly willing to listen to your ideas.''

Tasha wondered how the district had gotten into such trouble. She might not be too smart, but she knew someone had failed to plan well for the future.

For a moment the audience was stunned by the

size of their shortfall, then they began to make suggestions.

"We could take up a collection."

"There ain't that much spare cash in the whole town," another person countered.

"How about a hair-cutting marathon?" Harriet suggested. "Everybody could cough up ten bucks for the school."

From the risers, Winnie said, "You'd have to give haircuts to half of the population of Great Falls to raise enough money."

As individuals continued to make suggestions, Tasha noticed Cliff check his pager. He leaned toward her.

"I've got to call the office. I'll be right back."

She nodded and watched as he edged out of the row of seats and made his way to the back of the gym. Anxious that he might be called into a dangerous situation, her mouth went dry, and she forced her attention back to the subject of closing the school.

The state superintendent had turned the evening into a town meeting, allowing anyone to speak who wanted to. But soon, as all of the ideas for salvaging the school were shot down as being impractical, the audience members quieted. Tasha sensed the desperation around her, the loss of community pride at being unable to save their school. From somewhere deep inside an urge rose for her to do her part, to help Cliff and his son, and these people who were mostly strangers to her. Idly her mind shifted through ideas, landing on one that was truly bold and probably foolhardy.

"You could ask an international fashion designer to show his new designs here, in the heart of western America. That would bring the press and critics from all around the country, possibly the world. You could charge a hefty admission for tickets." She wasn't quite sure where the thought had come from or why she'd said anything, particularly at the precise moment when the room had gone silent except for her lone voice.

Everyone turned toward her. Even the children stared at her, their mouths agape.

Her cheeks heating under their scrutiny, she waited for someone to shoot down her idea as they had rejected every other possibility that had been offered.

No one said anything out loud. Instead they whispered among themselves, and Mr. Toomey consulted with the school board members in hushed voices, heads nodding.

Tasha mentally looked for a hole to crawl into. They hadn't even bothered to laugh at her dumb idea, just ignored it.

"Ms. Reynolds, isn't it?" Mr. Toomey asked.

She should have kept her big mouth shut. "Yes, sir."

"Stand up, please."

Now she felt as if she'd been called into the principal's office for some terrible misdeed. Desperately trying to hold onto her poise, she rose.

"Do you have the kind of connections that could

make a fashion show of that caliber possible here in Reilly's Gulch?''

My God, he was taking her idea seriously! ''I, uh, yes, sir, I know several important designers as well as a good many leading models. I think…I'd have to ask, of course.'' She mentally pictured the gym with a runway in the middle and realized this hall wouldn't be large enough to do a show justice. But the Cattlemen's Association facility next door was a much larger building, potentially a unique setting. ''I think if we combined haute couture with children's fashions, we'd have a clever show that would draw well. And our own children could be the models, working with the professionals,'' she added as more images came to mind.

The buzz of whispers increased in volume. Tasha wanted to sit down, but Toomey's stern gaze kept her upright like a naughty child who didn't dare run away.

''Ms. Reynolds,'' he asked, ''would you be able to ascertain the feasibility of your proposal by the next meeting of the school board?''

''I, uh, yes. I suppose I could.'' Or, as an alternative, she could pack up her daughter, her BMW and leave town in a hurry.

''Very well. I'm willing to delay my decision regarding closure of the school until you have an opportunity to assess your plan.''

''*My plan?*'' she asked, but her voice was drowned out by the cheering audience. ''No, wait—''

Right then Cliff slid back into the row of seats. "What's going on?" he asked.

"I think—" her mind stumbled "—I just volunteered to organize a fashion show to raise fifty thousand dollars to keep the school open for another year."

"Hey, that's a great idea." He leaned past Stevie to speak into her ear. "Look, the sheriff is coming by to pick me up in a minute. There's more rustling activity, in east county this time. We've got a chance to catch the suspects."

"That's good," she said absently, stunned by the enormity of what she'd agreed to do. Or *try* to do.

He handed her his truck keys. "You can drive a truck, can't you?"

She looked at him blankly. "You want me to drive Brute home?" A four-wheel-drive monster?

"I knew that's what you'd say." His lips twitched into a quick smile. "I'll be late. Don't wait up for me."

Bewildered by all that was happening, she managed to remind him to be careful.

And then he was gone, the meeting adjourned and dozens of people were crowding around her, volunteering to help or have their children be models. Even the school board chairman embraced her idea.

Tasha's stomach roiled. She'd never in her life organized anything more complicated than a birthday party for Melissa. What in heaven's name was she going to do when the whole town of Reilly's Gulch was suddenly relying on her to save their school?

THE SIREN SILENT on the four-wheel-drive police cruiser, Sheriff Colman rocketed along the dark county highway. Cliff checked his seat belt one more time. Granted, Larry knew these roads like he knew his wife's cooking, but Cliff wasn't eager to test the limits of his boss's reflexes if a deer decided to take an evening stroll across the road.

"I'd just as soon we arrived in one piece," he said, hoping Larry would get the hint.

He didn't. "Amos Thurman said he heard a truck going through his south section. Wouldn't be any reason for an eighteen-wheeler to be out that direction at night."

"It could have been kids with a souped-up pickup."

"Maybe. But I got a hunch it's not."

"Why's that? There's no full moon tonight." And that was when most of the rustling activity had taken place.

The road bent. Colman applied his brakes lightly, taking the curve at maximum speed. "No moon, but practically every rancher in the Reilly's Gulch school district is at the board meeting tonight. That leaves a lot of empty ranch houses around the county."

"Good point. And Amos has kids in school. They might have figured he'd be there, too."

"Yep. Except he pulled his back out a couple of days ago and can barely get out of bed. He sent his wife and kids, but he skipped the meeting."

Which would be why Amos hadn't gone to investigate the noise himself.

Cliff ran his hand over his face. As usual, he'd been up since early morning. The election campaign and his usual chores, on top of the weeks of roundup at the Double S, had left him short on sleep—that, and nightly dreams of Tasha that kept him awake.

He couldn't get their kiss out of his mind. Even now, just thinking about it, he was getting hard. Her sweet flavor lingered on his tongue, her sultry scent in the air around him. The tactile memory of her small breasts pressed against his chest dogged him from morning to night, his need to cup them with his hands a temptation he had barely resisted. It didn't matter that he was riding along at eighty miles an hour en route to a possible encounter with cattle rustlers. Tasha filled his mind.

That was dangerous, and not simply because a loss of concentration could cost him his life. He was beginning to care too much and so was Stevie. When Tasha left, both he and his son would pay a price.

The sheriff wheeled in the entrance to Amos's ranch, slowing as he approached the house.

Cliff scanned the landscape, undulating terrain that slowly rose toward the foothills of the Rocky Mountains. Starlight revealed no sign of an eighteen-wheeler and there wasn't much of anywhere to hide one. Nor had they passed a truck on the road getting here.

They got out of the cruiser and went up to the front door. When they knocked, Amos shouted for them to come in. He was laying on the couch, wearing a robe and slippers, a hot pad under his back.

"You spot 'em?" he asked.

"Not yet," Larry said. "How far away do you figure they were when you heard the truck?"

"Hard to tell. You know how sound carries funny at night. I'd guess a mile, maybe more. Probably the south pasture."

"We'll go take a look. Wanted you to know we were here so you wouldn't start taking potshots at us with that shotgun of yours."

Amos laughed, then winced when another pain zinged him. "I'll let you do any shooting that needs doing tonight, Sheriff."

It wasn't all that easy to drive around cattle country in the dark. The cruiser could hit a hole and break an axle, or get centered on a high rock. Larry kept his eyes on where they were going; Cliff worked the spotlight back and forth across the ground, trying to spot tire tracks or telltale signs that the grass had been flattened by the weight of an eighteen-wheeler. Better yet, he'd like to spot the truck.

It was a slow, painstaking and futile search in the dark.

Bone-jarring hours later they crossed the tracks, which led to a break in the fence they'd earlier missed as they sped by on the county road. There was no sign of the truck, which could have taken the road back to Reilly's Gulch or gone east to another road that cut north. From there the truck could have gone in any direction.

"Damn, these rustlers are good," Larry grumbled.

"They seem to know right where the cattle are grazing." Standing at the side of the road, Cliff studied the distinctive tire tracks in the beam of his flashlight. "And they're not greedy. They round up the cows that are easy, herd 'em into the truck and they're gone. From the signs I'd guess Amos lost twenty head. All neat and tidy, this was." And in this case, on a night when the chances of someone seeing or hearing them had been between zero and none if Amos hadn't been home.

Cliff didn't believe in coincidence. The perpetrators were locals and had known exactly where everyone else in the community would be tonight.

"Larry, I think we need to ask the State Police for help. If they'd run some helicopter patrols out this direction, maybe they'd be able to spot a big rig where it doesn't belong."

"Good idea. I'll call 'em in the morning."

"Of course, my son's friend, Ricky Monroe, might be right." Shoving his hands in his pockets, he looked up at the starlit sky. "We could be dealing with space aliens who are rustling our steers to feed their hungry families on some other planet."

"I don't think so, boy." The sheriff walked back across the field to the cruiser, his shoulders slumped with fatigue, his age showing for the first time Cliff could recall. The time was right for Larry to retire, which made it all the more crucial for Cliff to win the upcoming election.

IT WAS AFTER three o'clock when Cliff finally got home, his head fuzzy with fatigue. He'd been up

Play the
"LAS VEGAS"
GAME

Play the "LAS VEGAS" Game

and get

3 FREE GIFTS!

twenty-two hours straight. His body craved sleep like a thirsty man longed for water.

Taking his boots off in the kitchen, he walked quietly through the house. In the bedroom where he'd been sleeping for the past three years, he tossed his shirt aside and unzipped his pants, sliding them and his socks off all in the same motion, then rolled into bed. He exhaled with relief, letting weariness and sleep overtake him.

Tasha's scent teased him in his dreams. Her arm draped across his chest, her head resting comfortably on his shoulder, her body curling against the length of his. Pleasant dreams. If he'd had an ounce of energy left, the erotic sensation of a woman beside him would have aroused him from the sleep he so desperately needed. Instead, having a woman to hold soothed and comforted him. It had been a long time....

INSTINCTIVELY, Tasha snuggled into the warmth of the man beside her. The faint tapping noise she heard didn't bother her. Instead she relished the steady beat of his heart and the warm feel of his skin beneath her palm, conscious of a light covering of hair across his chest. She felt secure. Cherished. Infinitely at ease, as though she'd been lost for a long time and had finally come home.

The tapping became insistent. Closer. Louder. Jarring.

She squeezed her eyes more tightly closed against the press of sunlight on her eyelids. Morning, she realized. Time to get up and she wasn't anywhere near ready to give up the snug place she'd discovered.

It had taken her ages to get to sleep last night after the school board meeting. Her head had been spinning in a confusion of ideas to make the fashion show a success and myriad fears that she'd never be able to pull it off. She'd finally taken a pill to help her sleep.

The tapping grew irritating. Shifting slightly, she wished—

Everything about her stopped, even her breathing.

There was a man in her bed. A big man with a broad chest and muscular arms. A familiar man who smelled faintly of spicy aftershave mixed with the scent of sagebrush.

Her eyes flew open. She blinked at the bright sunlight, and her gaze focused, slamming into that of Winifred Bruhn standing outside the window. The shade was up, sheer curtains the only thing that prevented a clear view into the bedroom.

"Cliff!" she whispered sharply. Mortified, she tried to shake him awake. "Cliff, wake up! You're in the *wrong* bed!"

Chapter Eight

Cliff came awake with a start.

His normal morning arousal jerked to full alert with the brush of Tasha's delicate breast against his arm and the intimate swipe of her hand across his abdomen.

Tasha? Her hair tousled, her eyes wide with alarm. My God! He didn't remember—

"Would you *do* something," she whispered, scrambling under the covers, pulling them over her head. "She can see in the window!"

"I know you're in there!" Winifred's distinctive twang cut through Cliff's blur of sleep, and she pounded on the window.

He jackknifed to a sitting position, grateful the blanket hid his reaction to whatever Tasha was doing under the covers. "Winnie, what in hell are you doing out there?"

"I'm trying to interview you about the rustlers, and if you don't let me in, in about two seconds I'm coming in anyway. The press has a right to know what's going on. There's a freedom of information act, you know.''

''Let her in,'' Tasha pleaded, her voice muffled by the blankets. ''Get her away from the window. She'll see...''

Getting out of bed, he thanked God he'd worn his shorts to sleep in or Winnie would have gotten an X-rated view of his privates. As it was, he had to turn his back so she wouldn't catch sight of the telltale bulge that was only now receding.

''You stay here,'' he said to the lump under the covers. ''I'll get rid of her as quick as I can.'' Snatching up his pants from the floor, he pulled them on and grabbed his shirt.

''I'm coming!'' he shouted to Winnie.

He'd barely reached the hallway when Melissa and Stevie came running, barefoot and in their pajamas.

''What's all that noise, Uncle Cliff?''

''It woke us up,'' Stevie complained.

Hearing a groan, he shot a look at the mound of covers on the bed, then reached out to close the bedroom door. Damn, he'd never meant to embarrass Tasha. He couldn't even remember... Naw, it wasn't possible, but he'd been so damn tired. And he *had* dreamed.

''Just sheriff business, kids. No problem.''

''Is my mommy all right?'' Melissa asked.

''Sure, she's fine. I didn't want to wake her, is all,'' he ad-libbed. ''Why don't you guys go on back to bed. I've gotta talk to the press.'' Though thinking of Winifred Bruhn as a legitimate newspaper-woman was a stretch, at best.

TASHA HUDDLED under the covers until she was sure Winnie had moved away from the window. God, she couldn't believe that woman, of all people, had caught her in bed with Cliff.

Dear heaven, she couldn't believe it, either.

How could she have slept with a man of such potent masculinity without even knowing it? Without making love to him? And she hadn't. That, she would have remembered.

Getting up, she dressed hastily and tugged a brush through her unruly hair. Thank goodness Cliff had diverted the children. If *they* had caught her in bed with Cliff, the questions they'd ask wouldn't bear answering. She'd always tried to be so circumspect around Melissa.

Like a coward, she waited until she heard the back door slam shut and a car start, signaling Winnie's departure. Only then did Tasha leave the relative safety of the bedroom.

She found Cliff standing at the kitchen counter holding a mug of coffee, his khaki uniform shirt rumpled and only half buttoned, his feet bare. He looked sexy and virile, and her insides clenched with regret that they'd slept together without actually doing the deed. What a waste!

His gaze met hers, and her face heated as though this were a real morning after, that awkward moment when new lovers meet in the harsh light of day to discover if the flames of passion had been extinguished...or if the fires were only temporarily banked. For Tasha it would take only a tiny spark to kindle the desire she'd been trying to keep in check these past few weeks.

"Look, about last night," he began.

"Heck of a thing, huh?" She smiled, embarrassed, wishing he'd take her back into the bedroom and continue what they'd not even started last night.

"I was really beat when I got in—"

"I'd taken a sleeping pill. I didn't hear you." She shook her head. "In fact, I didn't hear a sound...till I heard Winnie pounding on the window."

He shoved away from the counter, mug in hand, the memory of vivid dreams coming back to him. "God, I can't believe I had you in bed and didn't do something about it. A man should never be that tired." He laughed at his own expense. "You must think my libido has taken an extended vacation along with my good sense, ending up in your bed like that."

"No, that's not what I think." She'd felt the iron hardness of his arousal as she'd scrambled under the covers, remembered his passion when he'd kissed her and had wanted him, foolish as that might be. Cliff had plenty of libido, as much as any man needed. And he aroused a sensual desire in her impossible to ignore.

"I'll promise you one thing." His eyes narrowed, his voice lowering to a husky whisper. "If I ever end up in bed with you again, the results will be a whole lot different."

His promise unnerved her. That was exactly what

she wanted, to make love with Cliff, but it was the wrong dream, the wrong man in the wrong place. Couldn't he see that? Yet she couldn't find the words to tell him because a secret part of her wanted that not to be true.

Turning away, she made a production of getting the orange juice out of the refrigerator and finding a glass in the cupboard.

"So what did Winnie want?" she asked.

"She had some questions about the rustling in east county last night. I filled her in with what we discovered…which was damn little."

Her hand paused in the act of pouring the juice. "Did she see us in bed together?"

"Yeah, I'm afraid so. She made a couple of snide comments about the public demanding morality these days in their elected officials. I'm afraid your name's going to get dragged through the mud. I'm sorry."

"What irony. Despite what she saw—or thinks she saw—it was an accident we were sleeping together. We didn't *do* anything. We're totally innocent."

"She's got a dirty mind."

"She's determined to ruin your reputation so her nephew will be elected sheriff."

"At this point, I'm more worried about your reputation than mine. I don't think there's a chance Bobby will beat me. Hell, he didn't even show up at the school board meeting last night to give his support to keep the school open. That's not going to win him any votes in this county. Forget that

Winifred said he'd had a bad case of stomach flu. He should have dragged himself there somehow.''

Taking her juice to the table, she sat down. Cliff might be right about the election, but she'd hate to risk his losing if Winnie stepped up her smear campaign. And the prospect of everyone in town learning she'd been sleeping with Cliff wasn't a pleasant one. Her sister wouldn't care—she'd been trying to play matchmaker all along. But Tasha hated the thought of the gossip reaching Melissa's ears.

She looked up to find Cliff studying her. Her breath ached in her chest, her throat nearly closing down, but she made herself speak anyway.

"I think it's time for Melissa and me to go back to New York."

"No, Mommy!" Melissa wailed, running into the kitchen in her pajamas from the living room where she'd obviously been eavesdropping. "I don't want to go home yet."

Stevie raced in right behind her, launching his sturdy young body into Tasha's lap. "Don't go, Aunt Tasha. Don't go!"

Dear heavens! How much had they heard? Or understood?

Hugging the boy with one arm and wrapping the other around her daughter, she gave them both a squeeze. Amazingly, tears blurred her vision. She'd always known she would be going home to New York, yet she hadn't realized how much it would hurt when the time came.

"You both knew this was only a vacation," she reminded the children gently.

"But you promised! Last night you said you'd do a fashion show for everybody," Melissa cried. "Stevie 'n me were going to be models together!"

"It's sorta like being in a ballet," Stevie explained solemnly. "Melissa told me."

"And you'd both be wonderful, but—"

Cliff knelt beside her, making it a four-way hug as he wrapped his arms around all of them. "I think you should keep your promise."

"But if the gossip—"

"We haven't done anything wrong. I don't think we ought to act like we have."

"What's gossip?" Melissa asked.

Cliff settled back on his haunches, answering Melissa directly. "It's when somebody is saying bad things about you that aren't true."

"A girl at school told everybody I peed in my pants when I didn't," Melissa said.

"And that wasn't very nice of her, was it?"

"Uh-uh."

"Well, if you and your mom stick around for a while so your mother has a chance to put on the fashion show, you're likely to hear things that aren't nice about her. And me, for that matter. Would it bother you to have people talking about your mother that way?"

"Cliff, she's too young to decide—"

"No, I'm not, Mommy. I know you're nice, and so is Uncle Cliff. If people say bad things about you, I'll just, just—"

"Stick out your tongue at 'em," Stevie contributed.

Tasha swallowed a sound that was half laugh, half sob. Dear heaven, what an adorable little boy he was. She could just love him to pieces, the kind of child any woman would want to mother.

"That's the idea, bucko." Grinning, Cliff ruffled his son's short hair. "Except maybe it'd be more polite if you just ignored what other people said. You know, silence can be a pretty potent weapon, too."

"Is it okay if I stick out my tongue when they're not looking?"

"That's splitting hairs, but yeah, if they're not looking, go for it."

"Cliff..." Tasha warned.

Unremorseful, he shrugged. "So do you think you should stick around just to prove ol' Winifred can't run you out of town? You did promise the school board...."

"Please, Mommy..."

"I wanna be a model. Melissa says I can."

Cliff gave Tasha one of his wicked grins. The man was relentless...or a fool. And the kids were as skilled at laying on guilt as any traditional Greek mother. But the truth was, she hated to buckle under pressure, and she'd been damned excited about trying to put on a haute couture fashion show in the wilds of Montana. What a kick that would be!

"All right," she agreed hesitantly. "But only if I'm sure my being here won't hurt your election chances."

Standing, Cliff hefted Melissa in his arms. "Your mom's a winner, Little Miss Goldilocks. She's gonna make Winnie look like the big bad wolf with a pie on her face.''

Tasha wasn't anywhere near that confident. She wasn't entirely sure she could get a designer to show his wares this far out of the mainstream market. But it would be a heck of a promotion hook. Surely there was someone. Maybe an up-and-comer. And she thought she knew just the woman who'd be willing to take the risk.

CLIFF FINISHED breakfast and went into the master bedroom to shower and change clothes. He had work to do. But as he stood in the middle of the room, he saw his surroundings more clearly than he had for years.

A framed picture of Yvonne sat on the night table beside his bed. Though he'd sent most of her things to a women's shelter in Great Falls, he hadn't brought himself to discard bottles of perfume, a fancy hand mirror, or her combs and brushes that she'd kept on her dresser. He simply hadn't had the courage to entirely wipe her memory from the room or her lingering scent.

He should have.

It was time to move on with his life. If he was ever going to bring another woman into his bed—and he fully intended to, if she was willing—he had to put Yvonne in the past where she belonged.

He scooped the perfume bottles into the trash can along with her brushes; her photo he slid into his sock drawer. There was no way he'd ever forget Yvonne. He'd loved her too much. But he had a life to lead. He thought she'd want him to get on with it.

Even knowing that, he had to swipe at the tears in his eyes. Perhaps because he'd loved one woman so much, he was capable of loving another with an equal, though different, intensity. He hoped to God that was true and that he'd be given the chance.

TWO DAYS LATER, while Cliff was saddling his horse for a morning ride with the children, he spotted Tasha running toward the corral, shouting and waving her hand. She ran the same way she walked, all graceful motion like water flowing down a fishing stream.

"Arletta says she'll do it!" She was up and over the corral fence before recognizing there were actually *horses* there and she came to an abrupt halt. Her cheeks were flushed with excitement, her hair windblown and her blue eyes sparkled.

Amused and intrigued by this energetic version of his sophisticated housekeeper, Cliff thumbed his Stetson up at an angle. "Arletta-who is going to do what?"

"Arletta, the fashion designer. That's the only name she goes by. I don't even know if she has a last name. Well, she must, I suppose, but I don't know what it is." Tasha finally took a breath. "She's very avant garde, definitely making a name for herself. And she's going to show her new winter line at *our* fashion show." Her grin was so broad, it practically went from ear to ear.

Mounted on Peaches, Melissa asked, "Do I get to wear an Arletta design, Mommy?"

"No, honey, Arletta only does women's fashions. We'll get somebody else for the children's clothes. That should be easy now that we've got Arletta."

Stevie pulled the cinch tight on his saddle like an old pro. "I don't wanna wear a dress, anyway. I'm a boy."

Cliff chuckled and grinned at Tasha, feeling as proud as the proverbial peacock about her success. "Congratulations! I knew you could do it."

"Only because Arletta has her designs ready to go and was looking for a new angle. When I talked to Mr. Toomey on the phone, he said the school district has to have the money in hand before the new fiscal year starts. And Arletta wants to have her show in *two* weeks because all the other designers will get ahead of her if she doesn't. Do you know how much needs to be done? I'll never be able to—"

"You'll get it done. You're one hell of a good organizer."

She looked at him blankly. "Me? You think I'm a good organizer?"

"She made me organize my underwear drawer once," Melissa interjected.

"Tasha, honey," Cliff said, "I don't know anybody who could have organized my campaign better, getting letters sent out, keeping track of the money coming in and scheduling my speaking dates. And to begin with, you didn't know squat about campaigning. You know a lot more than that about putting on a fashion show, I'd venture. You'll be great.''

She appeared more stunned than pleased by his praise. Speechless. So he decided to take advantage of the moment.

''In fact, I'm so sure you'll do a great job, I think you need a reward.'' He slid his arm around her waist. ''You're going for a ride with us to celebrate.''

The kids cheered, and Stevie mounted Star Song.

Tasha's eyes grew wide. ''I can't—''

He lifted her easily, his other arm under her legs, and placed her on Sunny Boy's saddle. She grabbed for the saddle horn as if it were a life preserver and she was faced with the prospect of drowning.

''Cliff! I can't ride your horse! He's too—''

''Don't sweat it. We're going to ride double.''

''What?'' she gasped.

''It's better than my saddling Henry.''

Placing his boot in the stirrup, he mounted behind her, lifting her so she settled into his lap. Only then, when he felt the sweet curve of her buttocks, his body reacting with a swiftness that left him breathless, did it occur to him this might not be a smart idea. Taking the reins in one hand, he hooked his arm around her middle. She leaned back into him, fitting like a cup to a saucer. And she was that delicate, as fragile as porcelain, yet he sensed she had a steely strength she'd never fully recognized.

''Son, can you get the gate for us?''

''Sure.''

Stevie reined his horse around and trotted to the

corral gate. He had to lean halfway out of the saddle to lift the bar, but he did it as well as any full-grown cowboy would. The kid was a natural, and Cliff suddenly realized how quickly his son was growing up. He'd always wanted a big family, probably a subconscious urge to make up for the fact he had no blood relatives except Bryant. Then Yvonne had died....

His arm tightened more firmly around Tasha. "You ready?"

A shudder rippled through her slender body, which could have been because of her fear of horses or for some other reason. Cliff wasn't sure. He only knew she felt good in his arms.

"Yes," she whispered.

The morning air was still and fragrant with the scent of sage and wildflowers, the sky a crystalline blue. Like Tasha's eyes, Cliff thought, though he'd seen those same eyes turn dark with arousal when he'd kissed her. The vibrant grass of spring reached toward the sun, as eager as a virgin in search of her first taste of passion. Despite the fact Tasha had once been married and had borne a child, Cliff thought of her like that. Eager and not fully aware of the possibilities. Of what they could be together.

He picked a trail that wandered along the edge of a winter creek still silver with the flow of snow melt from the distant mountains. Meadowlarks sang a mating song, darting from one perch to another. Butterflies flitted from flower to flower; bees hummed as they gathered the first honey of spring.

"You know I have a million things to do," Tasha said.

He glanced over his shoulder to be sure the kids were all right, their horses following along single file behind him. "But you're enjoying this, aren't you?"

"Hmmm, as much as a rational person can enjoy being at the whim of a thousand-pound beast who could throw her off at the least little provocation."

He chuckled and rubbed his cheek against her hair, silky and smelling faintly of sultry tropical promises. "I don't weigh anywhere near that much."

"Oh, you..." She elbowed him in the stomach. "You know what I mean."

For the first time in all the riding lessons he'd given her, he sensed her relax. That was remarkable progress for a woman who'd been so terrified of horses.

"Here, you take the reins," he said.

"No, I don't want to—"

He tucked the reins into her hand. "You're in charge, sweetheart. Anything you want him to do, he'll do. I promise."

Automatically Tasha's fingers closed around the leather strips and she felt a moment of panic. How could she possibly control this huge animal? But she realized Cliff was right there with her. He wouldn't let anything go awry. And the slow easy walk of the horse, almost a rocking motion, with Cliff holding her so firmly, comforted her. At the same time she felt aroused, her nerve endings responding to sensual messages that had her on edge for reasons unrelated to her fear of horses.

It had taken all her willpower the past two nights not to give up her assigned bed and seek Cliff's instead. Only the thought of how much damage she'd already done—inadvertently—to Cliff's election campaign had kept her in her own bed, albeit sleepless for most of the night. The memory of waking in his arms, of how much she wished they had made love, was as effective as a dozen cups of coffee to keep her awake.

Stevie trotted up beside them. "Can we ride over to the main ranch and see Unka Bry?"

"Oh, no, I can't," Tasha said, the boy's question bringing her back to reality. "I've got to arrange accommodations for the models. There'll be five or six of them."

Cliff laughed. "Bet there are some hired hands around who'd be happy to share their bunkhouse with a model or two."

Tasha ignored him, her mind whirling with details that needed to get done. "The press has to be notified, and I've got to take a look at the Cattlemen's Association building to see if that would work better for the show than the school gym."

"Guess the answer's no, bucko. The lady needs to get back to work."

"Melissa and me could go on our own. I know the way."

Quickly, Tasha shook her head. "Not a chance, young man. You and Melissa are both too young to go riding off on your own like that." She wasn't *that* comfortable with the idea of trusting a horse, particularly with Melissa's life and limb.

"Ah, gee—"

"I'm not a baby," Melissa protested.

Cliff took the reins from Tasha, turning the horse back toward his house, which was still visible in the distance. "Race ya home, kids!"

The horse leaped forward. Tasha screamed and grabbed for the saddle horn.

They were up to full speed in an instant, the ground flying past them as the horse lengthened his stride. The wind blew in Tasha's face; her hair whipped free, teasing at her cheeks. Fear and excitement pumped adrenaline through her veins.

"Cliff, you're going to get us killed!"

"Naw, you're safe with me, Goldilocks. I promise." His low, husky laughter sent goose bumps speeding down her spine.

Tasha wasn't sure that was a promise Cliff could keep, nor was she sure she wanted him to. Right now she felt reckless, eager to succumb to temptation. Eager to surrender to what she knew both of them wanted.

She leaned back into him, letting his strong thighs gentle her ride, his chest cushion her, his arms hold and protect her. Her body became one with his, adjusting easily to the movement of the horse. She found his rhythm, matched it. Closing her eyes, she let the sensation of them together sweep through her.

The ride was over too soon.

She opened her eyes as he reined to a stop near

the house. Ella was standing beside her pickup holding a newspaper to shade her eyes from the sun.

"I can't believe my little sister is riding a horse," she said.

Cliff dismounted and helped Tasha down, waving the youngsters on toward the corral.

"She just needs a little personalized coaching," he said with a grin.

Tasha's legs were wobbly, her body overheated. She felt needy, all right, but not for classes in horseback riding.

Giving Ella a hug, she said, "Hey, Sis, what brings you out on a day like this?"

"I was in town getting a few things and picked up a copy of today's *Register*." Frowning, she handed Tasha the newspaper. "I thought you'd both want to see it."

The headline splashed across the front page read, Character An Issue In Sheriff Race.

Chapter Nine

Cliff dropped Sunny Boy's reins to the ground, knowing the horse would stay put, and took the paper from Ella. The more he read, the angrier he got. Finally he swore out loud.

Tasha placed a calming hand on his arm. Her fingernails were shorter than they had been when she'd arrived in Montana, the polish clear. He'd liked seeing them raspberry. He'd grown used to her sharkskin boots, too, however inappropriate they were in ranch country.

"We knew Winnie would print something like this," she said.

"We ought to sue her for slander. Defamation of character. Something. She's got no right to go around printing lies like this."

"By the time you could file a lawsuit, the election would be over."

Ella looked incredulous, her eyes rounding behind her big glasses. "You mean it's not true? That you two aren't...I mean...you know."

Cliff wanted to say *not yet,* but Tasha spoke first.

"Winnie caught us in a compromising position and jumped to the wrong conclusion."

She was so damn cool, it annoyed him. Why wasn't she angry that Winnie was attacking her reputation, too? The answer was obvious. *She didn't plan to stay in Reilly's Gulch.*

The kids, who'd hitched their horses to the corral fence, came running up. "Hi, Aunt Ella," they chorused.

"Hi, you two." She gave them both hugs. "Did you have a nice ride?"

"We wanted to come see you," Stevie said.

"Where's Jason?" Melissa peered into the truck.

"He's at home with his daddy. In fact, I've really got to go. Bryant gets nervous if I leave him alone with Jason too long. I just wanted to bring that by to you." She nodded to the newspaper Cliff still held. "Thanks for not shooting the messenger."

"Can't say there isn't someone else I'd like to shoot," Cliff grumbled.

After saying their goodbyes, Cliff, Tasha and the children moved out of the way so Ella could turn the truck around.

"Is something wrong?" Melissa asked, gazing up at Cliff and her mother.

Instinctively, Cliff rested his hand on the child's shoulder. "Remember when we talked about people saying bad things about your mom and me?"

She nodded solemnly, wise for her age.

"Well, it's started." He showed her the newspaper.

Tasha took it away from her. "Anybody around here interested in some lunch?"

"I am," Stevie shouted.

Cliff knew Tasha was more bothered by the article than she wanted to let on. Under usual circumstances she never thought about food and rarely volunteered to fix a meal. Eating was low on her priority list; he suspected protecting her daughter was way up there on top. An admirable trait, he admitted, wishing she wasn't so set on returning to New York.

TASHA LEFT the children home with Cliff after lunch and headed for Sal's Bar and Grill. There was only one pickup parked out front. When she shoved through the old-fashioned saloon swinging doors, she thought the place was empty—empty except for the lingering smell of cigarettes and hops.

In the dim light, she made her way through a maze of tables and chairs that butted up against a small dance floor.

"Well, hello there, sweetheart."

Startled, she whirled toward the stranger sitting at the bar.

"Darned if you aren't that little piece of fluff Deputy Swain's been shacking up with. Not that I blame him, mind. You are some kind of babe. I'll give him points for good taste."

Tasha bristled. Of all the names she could think of, she hated being called babe the most.

Lifting her chin, she gave the stranger a hard look. About thirty-five, he had a narrow face and a slender physique, his thinning hair he wore in a brush cut. He seemed vaguely familiar.

Recognition slammed into her like a mugger on Forty-Second Street. ''You're Bobby Bruhn.''

''One and the same, sweetlin'.'' He pulled out the bar stool next to him. ''How 'bout joining me for a beer?''

''No, thank you,'' she said curtly. *I'd rather eat snails!* ''I was looking for Sal.''

''In her office watchin' her soaps, like she always does this time of day.''

She scanned the barroom for something that looked like an entrance to the office.

He took a swig of beer right from the bottle. ''Course, she don't like her soaps interrupted so you might as well hang around with me till they're all done. I can be real good company when I put my mind to it.''

His salacious grin was the same sort Tasha imagined men wore when they were watching strippers. That was how she felt—dirty and stripped naked by his beady little eyes.

''I think I'd prefer the company of a mule, Mr. Bruhn.'' Coolly, she turned away, walking with exaggerated indifference toward the open door she'd spotted and what she hoped was Sal's office.

His laughter followed her, sending shivers of distaste down her spine. Who in their right mind would vote for a man like that for sheriff? Certainly no woman she'd ever known.

Sal was indeed concentrating on a small television set and the sharp images of characters in emotional turmoil. Love and betrayal; would he or wouldn't he do the right thing? Not a single brassy-blond hair on Sal's head moved and she didn't even look up when Tasha slipped into the room. Still, Tasha was glad of a safe refuge from Bobby Bruhn's crude attentions.

While she waited for Sal to come out of her soap-opera-induced coma, Tasha examined the office with amused interest. Every level space in the room was occupied. Piles of papers and magazines were stacked everywhere, including on top of unopened cartons of liquor. Little wonder Sal had hired Ella to do her bookkeeping. Organizing paperwork was obviously not the woman's strong suit.

Finally the music swelled and the credits rolled on the TV. Sal leaned back in her creaking, wooden desk chair, swiveling around, muttering to herself, "Those folks are the most—" She spotted Tasha. "Oh, my Lord! I didn't hear you come in!"

"You were pretty engrossed," Tasha conceded with a smile.

"I do get a little wrapped up in it...." She leaned forward, her expression concerned. She wore a stenciled T-shirt with the sleeves ripped out, revealing arms as thick as Tasha's thighs. "How are you, honey?"

Tasha suspected Sal's heart matched her mammoth size, and she probably wore it on her sleeve more often than not, no matter what kind of shirt she slipped on. "I'm fine."

"You and Cliff not letting Winnie get to you?"

Despite her best efforts to control it, a blush stole

up Tasha's cheeks. People might have thought ill of her in the past or questioned her morals, but they'd never said it in print. "Freedom of the press, I suppose."

"Bah! She's a witch, that one. I'd cancel my advertising except she's got a monopoly going. Her yellow rag is the only way I can let folks know what bands are playing here Saturday nights. Damndest thing! Same problem for the grocery 'n feed stores in town. If we don't advertise, folks forget about us and hump themselves all the way to Great Falls for what they need. If I thought it would help you and Cliff—"

"It's all right." Tasha waved off her concern. "I actually came by because I need to make room reservations."

Sal arched her plucked eyebrows. "You need a room?"

Tasha laughed. "No, Cliff hasn't thrown me out yet. Though if I don't learn how to iron his uniform shirts better, he might do just that. What I do need are rooms for the fashion models and designer who'll be doing the show for the school district."

"You got somebody?" Sal's smile broadened.

"Designs by Arletta. Very avant garde." She gave Sal the dates she'd need and the number of rooms.

"Honey, this place of mine and the rooms upstairs ain't exactly fancy. I'm not sure—"

"It's the only place in town, Sal. I wanted to book enough rooms now before the press and fashion critics get wind of the show. When that happens, you'll be overwhelmed with reservations.''

Sal looked at her, dumbfounded. ''The press?''

''I'd jack up my prices, if I were you. *After* you make me a really good deal.''

Her booming laughter rocketed around the room. ''You got it, honey. And I'm gonna throw the biggest party this little ol' town has ever seen. Once the local cowboys hear I've got New York models staying here, there'll be standing room only. Honey, I do believe you just made my day. Hell, you've probably made my whole year!''

Within minutes they had agreed to the number of rooms Arletta and the crew from New York would need, the price imminently fair. Then Tasha said, ''We're going to need music, too. Something like a piano trio.''

Sal looked taken aback. ''Three pianos?''

''No, a piano plus a violin and cello. Something like that.''

She choked on another laugh. ''I'm afraid you're barking up the wrong tree, looking for them kind of musicians around here. We've got combos that play loud and bad, but it don't matter because everybody's havin' too good a time two-stepping.''

Well, of course, Tasha should have realized that. And Arletta had said she was going to emphasize the great outdoors, independence and all that the West stood for. The fast pace of two-stepping would be perfect.

With Arletta's authorization and the designer's credit card backing her, Tasha arranged for Sal to hire the best combo available, then she headed for home.

To the west, clouds were building over the mountains and she wondered if they'd get rain. For the past week the early summer storms had passed north of Reilly's Gulch, but she didn't imagine their luck would last forever.

She still had to arrange for rental chairs and risers for a runway, items she'd have to get from Great Falls. With luck she could get the PTA ladies to drape a little bunting around, making the large auditorium at the Cattlemen's Association look festive. She'd have to check on the speaker system, assuming there was one, decide where the models would change costumes.

A million details were racing through her head as she pulled into Cliff's driveway, only to find it blocked by an oversize van with the name of the only church in town stenciled on the side.

Why, she wondered, would church people be calling on Cliff? Maybe something about the election...

She pulled her BMW off to the side of the driveway, parked in the low weeds and walked to the back door, letting herself into the kitchen. Hearing voices in the living room, she eased in that direction. Two women and a man were standing in the center of the room talking with Cliff. Tasha mentally groaned when she saw the piles of clean laundry which she'd neglected to fold and put away filling every chair. Not a good recommendation for her skills as a housekeeper, she thought grimly. Though it was Cliff's own fault for dragging her off horse-back riding that morning.

Stepping into the room, she said, "Here, let me get these things out of your way—"

"Please don't trouble yourself, Ms. Reynolds," the gentleman said, his distinctive collar marking him as the local preacher. "We don't plan to stay long, do we, ladies?"

"Not at all," agreed the shorter and stouter of the two women.

"We only wanted to give you a proper welcome to the community," the taller one said.

Together the two women looked like the Mutt and Jeff cartoon characters, one long and beak-nosed, the other as round as a teapot.

As Cliff introduced the trio, his voice taut, a muscle flexing at his jaw, Tasha got an uncomfortable feeling their visitors had an agenda she wasn't going to like. Preacher Goodfellow, Millicent Walker and Flo Strickland looked like they were executioners here to counsel the condemned—namely her.

"Now, we're not ones to cast the first stone," the preacher assured her, his voice condescending.

"But we are, naturally, concerned about appearances," Millicent added.

"And the well-being of the children. Young minds are so easily influenced, don't you know," Flo said.

Tasha's temper started a slow simmer. "Just what are you trying to say?"

Cliff said, "They're saying they read the newspaper. They're thinking of voting for Bruhn because of the lies Winnie wrote unless I clean up my act.''

''Winifred is a member of my congregation, a fine woman—''

''Winnie is a—''

Stopping Cliff's tirade by holding up her hand, Tasha said, ''People in this county would actually vote for Bobby Bruhn because of what she printed in the *Register?* I met the man today and I can't believe anyone would be that...stupid!''

''You met Bobby?'' Cliff asked.

Tasha nodded. ''At Sal's—drinking his lunch, I surmised. Not exactly a good recommendation for a sheriff's candidate.''

Flo lifted her narrow nose. ''The article certainly poses some questions that need answering. We're here out of the goodness of our hearts to offer you, Ms. Reynolds, a place to stay out of temptation's reach—that's if you don't care to stay at your sister's. As a New Yorker, you may not understand how to conduct yourself in a small town.''

Millicent continued, ''Clifford, we understand the difficulties of a single father finding child care. The ladies of the congregation are willing to take turns baby-sitting your Stevie until Sophia returns or other, more *proper* arrangements can be made.''

''You sure never offered before,'' Cliff snapped.

''We feel this is a very generous offer on the part of the—'' The preacher stopped midsentence when Cliff took him by the arm.

''Thanks for dropping by, Reverend.'' Forcefully, Cliff ushered him to the front door. ''You, too, ladies. But I assure you I'm perfectly happy with the child care arrangements I've already made. I don't appreciate you insulting a good friend of mine, and I don't intend to change anything because of what you or anybody else in the county says.'' Unsmiling, he held open the door. ''Have a good day.''

Millicent and Flo huffed in unison, sweeping past the preacher and out the door.

''I would urge caution,'' the preacher warned Cliff. ''Bobby Bruhn may not be the ideal candidate for sheriff, but I wouldn't want to anger the women in the community, if I were you.''

When Cliff didn't respond, the preacher left. Cliff carefully closed the door behind him, though Tasha suspected it cost him not to slam it.

Folding her arms across her chest, she struggled to control the fury threatening to turn her into a shrew.

''Where are the children?'' she asked with forced calmness.

He plowed his fingers through his hair. ''When I realized what those people wanted, I sent them out to check on the horses.''

''Thank you.'' At least her daughter hadn't heard the none-too-subtle accusations of her mother's immorality. Or Cliff's.

''I'm sorry you had to go through that. I was hoping to get rid of them before you got home.''

''Home? I'd say those people made it quite clear this *isn't* my home.'' And never would be; they'd always think of her as an outsider.

Picking up a pair of Stevie's jeans from the pile

of laundry, she snapped the wrinkles out and folded them. Her hands were shaking with anger and the unfairness of it all.

"Here, let me help." He picked one of Melissa's tops, folding it neatly.

"Don't you have to get ready for work?" He was still dressed in his blue work shirt and jeans, his sexy cowboy apparel, and it was almost time for him to transform himself into a sexy officer of the law. She still couldn't decide which image she preferred. *Naked and in bed with her* sounded like a good option, too.

"I called the sheriff after lunch. I'm taking the next couple of weeks off, until after the election."

She glanced at him. "Is that wise?"

"I've got too much to do and so do you, now that you've got the fashion show to plan."

He fingered her cotton nightgown before folding and smoothing it flat. She could almost feel his large, callused hands caressing her instead, and wondered if maybe the local parishioners weren't right. Succumbing to temptation seemed all too likely if she stayed. But she couldn't leave now, not with the fashion show scheduled so soon. She'd made a commitment not only to the town but to Arletta as well.

"So how'd it go with Sal?" Cliff asked, adding a pair of bikini underwear to the growing pile of her clothes.

"Fine. She gave me a good price for the rooms."

He paused longer with the wisp of fabric that was her bra. Her nipples puckered on their own. Her throat tightened on what needed to be said.

"Cliff, I don't know if it will be soon enough to help your election, but after the fashion show is over, Melissa and I will be leaving."

His hand closed around her bra, crumpling it in his fist, and he nodded.

THE STORM ARRIVED after the children had gone to bed. Restless, Tasha put on a jacket and went outside to sit on the porch swing, watching the distant flashes of lightning. The branches of the willow tree in the front yard whipped back and forth as though they were trying to escape the oncoming storm. Wind-driven raindrops slanted through the column of light cast from the living room window.

Tasha hunkered down further into her jacket, pulling the collar up around her ears. Cliff had gone to a meeting in a neighboring town, determined to shake every voter's hand he could find.

There was an intimacy to the wind and rain, different from the storms she'd experienced from the relative safety of her condo in a city crowded with millions of people. Here it was one-on-one. A challenge. In the worst of times, Tasha knew a Montana storm could be life-threatening. This milder version was exhilarating, as though the electricity that arced from one cloud to another was also touching her. Her body tingled with it...and with unfulfilled desire.

The rain and wind eased as the headlights of Cliff's truck swept across the porch, making Tasha squint against the brightness. He parked and jogged easily through the rain. He wore a short leather jacket over a Western-cut shirt that hugged his shoulders, and slacks with angled pockets; his dressy Stetson rode low on his forehead. He looked like a cowboy ready and willing to go dancing with his favorite girl.

Tasha wished desperately she could be that girl, and knew it wasn't in the cards. In a little more than two weeks she'd be in her car heading back to New York, to the life where she belonged.

With his long legs, he took the porch steps all in one leap.

"Hey, you look cold." He took off his hat and slapped it on his thigh, dislodging a few drops of water.

"A little," she conceded. Though mostly the cold she felt was on the inside, not from the changing weather.

"How 'bout I warm you up." He sat down next to her, rocking the swing into motion. The chains creaked and the seat tipped slightly in his direction.

She shivered, and he looped his arm around her. "How was the meeting?" she asked.

"Okay, I guess."

"They'd seen the newspaper article, I gather."

"There were a few questions. Nothing I couldn't handle."

"If it weren't for me, you wouldn't have to *handle* anything."

"If it weren't for you, I would have had to take Stevie with me to the meeting. Or not go at all." With his hand, he gently tugged her head down to his shoulder. "You know, it galls the hell out of me that we're accused of sleeping together when we're not. I'm tempted to do it just so Preacher Goodfellow and his ladies wouldn't be put in a position of believing a lie.''

Tasha went very still. The branches of the willow tree had quieted and the rain was falling more gently now. But her heart was racing as if she'd spent the past hour running from the storm. And mentally she had been.

''Just because you're falsely accused of something, doesn't make it right to do it anyway in order to prove you can.''

''That's not why I want to make love to you and you know it.''

She didn't have time to object as he lifted her chin and brought his mouth down over hers. Her desire, already charged by the electricity of the storm, flared brightly. She felt like a thief, greedy to steal this time in Cliff's arms. What would a few minutes, an hour, matter? Their suspected affair had been trumpeted in bold headlines. People tended to believe what they read, even when it was a lie. She could...for a little while...make it the truth, and then she would leave Montana behind.

A hoarse, strangled cry rose in her throat. She kissed him back, shocked by the fierceness of her own desire. Her determination to steal what she could before she was forced to leave—for his sake as well as her own.

His fingers were at her nape; his lips moved, caressing her jaw, her throat, the hollow above her breasts. She ached for him. Wanted him with a passion that had always eluded her.

A gust of wind shook the tree again, rattling the limbs together like the brush of silk on silk. In the barn, a horse nickered softly as though in response to the creaking swing.

"Cliff, could we go inside?" Her voice was breathless. She couldn't help it. Every breath she drew rasped loudly, magnified a thousand times in the quiet of the dark countryside .

"My pleasure, Ms. Goldilocks." He scooped her up in his arms.

She clung to him, felt his muscles flex, buried her face in the crook of his neck. His spicy aftershave teased at her senses. She nipped lightly, wanting to taste him.

Shoving the door open, he carried her inside and kicked the door shut behind them.

"The children," she whispered. "They might wake—"

"There's a lock on the master bedroom door. They won't bother us."

She'd never been in the master bedroom; she'd made that room off-limits. But she'd seen inside, the big bed and the simple but elegant oak furniture. A large oval hooked rug on the hardwood floor. A room in the Western style suitable for a big man, perfect for a cowboy and his bride. A room where Cliff had lain with his wife, where they had loved and made a baby together.

"Cliff, are you sure?"

"About what?" He carried her inside. "Making love to you? Damn right, I'm sure."

"No, this room. You and your wife—"

He set her on her feet and framed her face with his hands, looking deeply into her eyes. The lamp on the bedside table cast a subdued light in the room, golden and sensual.

"There aren't any ghosts here, Tasha, if that's what you're worried about. They left when I wasn't looking. It's just you and me, and whatever we choose to do."

At her almost imperceptible nod of acquiescence, he closed the door and locked it.

Her legs were trembling so badly, she wasn't sure they'd be able to hold her upright. It wasn't as if this was her first time, a nervous adolescent embarking on uncharted waters. But she wanted this…wanted Cliff more than she'd wanted any man in her life. The realization stunned her.

He tugged her blouse from her waistband, his hands shaking almost as much as her legs as he shoved her top over her shoulders, trapping her arms.

"Do you know I almost lost it this afternoon trying to fold your bra?" He leaned forward and licked his tongue across the sheer fabric over her already pebbled nipple. "You're so delicate, so perfect."

So sensitive. She nearly shattered into a thousand pieces and all he'd done was touch her breast once with his tongue. Heat pooled in her lower body, luscious and liquid. How much more thrilling would it be when he loved her entirely? Deeply. She could barely stand the anticipation. Or the waiting.

Urgency drove her now. She set to work baring his chest to her touch, her eager exploration of muscle and sinew, crisp hair over warm flesh.

"Nice," she murmured, then gasped as her bra fell free and he cupped both breasts in his hands.

"Thank you. I quite agree."

The remainder of their clothes came off in a flurry. Boots. Pants. All dropped carelessly to the floor. Then his hand slipped beneath the waistband of her undies, probing until he found her damp and ready.

"I think I'm ready to make a deal with you," he whispered, his voice husky with wanting.

"Hmm." She'd agree to anything he asked. Anything at all.

"I get to fold your undies any time I want. You've got the sexiest—"

She giggled. *Giggled!* A sophisticated New York fashion model and she'd actually laughed in the middle of their foreplay.

He took advantage of her mortification by pulling her down onto the bed with him. Then it wasn't a laughing matter at all.

The rhythm of her breathing altered as he rose above her. He was a big man. All over. And she wondered how she'd ever accommodate him.

But she needn't have worried. He filled her slowly, gently, stretching her taut until she thought she might burst. But her body accepted him. As did her heart.

He paused, buried deep inside her, holding himself above her as though this moment meant as much to him as it did to her. And then he began a slow, steady stroking. Much too slow, in her view. She arched to him, trying to take it faster.

"Easy, Goldilocks. This is the best bed in the house."

It was. And he was the best lover. But that didn't ease her impatience. She dug her fingers into his shoulders, urging him on. Something in her was trying to break free. Something wonderful, if only he'd go a little faster, stroke a little deeper.

She wanted to scream; she wanted to cry. "Please…"

A shudder passed through him. "You're making me crazy."

"Do you have any idea what you're doing to—" She squeezed her eyes shut as he thrust more deeply and the tension mounted. It was too much, too wonderful. Her mouth opened with a scream, which he trapped as he kissed her, her body pulsing toward fulfillment.

A moment later she swallowed his cry of pleasure when he surged within her.

She dozed for a while. She couldn't be sure how long. Then he took her again. Easily. Gently. Afterward she collapsed into a sleep more sound than she had slept in years.

SHE WOKE the next morning at dawn as Cliff was leaving the bed to start his day. Stretching, muscles aching that hadn't been used in a long time, she cherished the tenderness of each part of her body. Cherished the time she had stolen to be with Cliff.

But the children would be up soon. Life would go on. For her, a fashion show to plan; for Cliff, an election to win. But she'd be gone before the votes were cast. There wouldn't be any last-minute mud-slinging to stain his reputation.

Her heart squeezed painfully in her chest. She'd see to that.

Chapter Ten

Cliff had a moment of panic when he saw the bed was empty. He hadn't been gone long....

Then he realized Tasha probably didn't want the kids to catch them in bed together—or even behind a locked door. Too many questions. Chances were good neither he nor Tasha had all the answers yet.

His gut clenched as he pulled on a clean work shirt.

Despite the mind-bending sex last night, nothing had changed. So far as he knew, Tasha still intended to return to New York. The fact that she was so excited about planning the fashion show in Reilly's Gulch ought to tell him she was in a career she loved. She'd sure never gotten that pumped up over ironing his shirts.

Hell, the first thing he'd do when he was elected sheriff was to switch the department's official uniforms to something wash-and-wear!

Which wouldn't mean much if she still preferred New York over Montana. She'd still leave him.

Unless...

He finished dressing and hurried downstairs, made the coffee and put the oatmeal on to cook. He waited anxiously for Tasha to show up. There was one thing that might sway the balance, keeping her here with him.

Sure, he'd been foolish. Damn careless. Even irresponsible. And for the first time he secretly hoped he'd have to pay a price for being so thoughtless of a woman's well-being.

She came into the kitchen dressed in a deceptively simple skirt and blouse, the subdued color emphasizing the silver-gold of her hair, which she'd piled on top of her head in a sophisticated swirl. Gold hoop earrings and a matching gold necklace drew attention to the slender column of her neck; the variegated belt cinching her narrow waist would attract the eye of any man passing within a hundred feet. Her platform heels brought her to eye level with Cliff, though she averted her gaze.

"I take it you're not going riding this morning," he said, admiring the sway of her softly pleated skirt as she walked.

She made a beeline for the coffeepot. "I need to go into Great Falls. I want to talk with the fashion editor of the paper and drop by Hennessey's Department Store to talk with the women's wear buyer and the head of the children's department." She glanced up from the mug of coffee she'd poured. "I don't know what your schedule is today. If you're not available to watch the children, I can take them with me."

"I'm available."

"I should be back before dinner." She slipped a slice of bread into the toaster.

"Tasha…"

"I'm going to check on the rental company, too. It's important the audience chairs are comfortable, not those awful metal things."

"We need to talk about last night."

A faint blush colored her cheeks, but she still didn't look at him. "It was wonderful. Thank you."

Thank you? What the hell was going on? "That's all you've got to say? People *thank* someone for opening a door."

The toast popped up. "I guess I'm not very good at mornings after. I'm sorry. It was…" She studied the toast as if she were memorizing the arrangement of the grains of wheat. "You were—"

He crossed the room in two strides and took her by the shoulders, turning her toward him. He lifted her chin with the tip of his finger, forcing her to look at him. "It was the best night of sex I've ever had. You are the most responsive lover I can imagine. You were terrific, and what I really want is to take you back to the bedroom, lock the door again and stay there all day making love to you."

"Me, too," she whispered, her eyes sad and serious.

His lips twitched into a grin. "That's better. You had me worried there for a minute. I thought maybe I didn't measure up to all those fancy dudes in New York."

"You measure up just fine."

"There is one little problem. We didn't use any protection."

She studied him, that cute little inverted V forming between her brows. "I don't have a disease, if that's what you're asking."

"Tasha, honey, that thought didn't cross my mind. But you could be pregnant."

"No." Her voice was so soft, he could barely hear her response.

"It's a safe time of month?"

"I'm safe. You don't have to worry."

"I wasn't exactly worried." In fact, he felt a sharp stab of disappointment that she didn't think she'd be pregnant, which wasn't a very responsible reaction. He and Tasha hadn't discussed having children. He had no idea how she felt about having more kids, except he knew she was a terrific mom and any children she gave birth to would be pretty special. And he liked the idea of being their dad. "But if it did happen, I mean if you did happen to be pregnant after last night, I want you to know I'll be there for you...and the baby."

Tears suddenly sheened her eyes and she shook her head. "I won't be pregnant."

She slipped away from him, like sand trickling through his fingers, and left him standing in the kitchen wondering what had made her cry and why she hadn't bothered to eat her toast.

Obviously he'd handled their "morning after" conversation all wrong. Since the only woman he'd ever been with until last night had been Yvonne, he didn't have much experience at this sort of thing.

Somehow he'd blown it. Maybe he'd misread Tasha. Having more kids might not be a great idea for a woman whose career depended upon keeping her figure.

A career she could only pursue in New York, not in a remote cattle ranching county in Montana.

FOR THE NEXT two weeks, Tasha filled every moment of her time with plans for the fashion show. She didn't allow herself to think about Cliff, about the way he had loved her and how much she wanted him to love her again. She only survived the nights alone in her bed by being so bone-tired, she fell into an exhausted sleep the moment her head hit the pillow.

But she did dream. Achingly erotic dreams that always featured Cliff as her lover.

Finally the day of the fashion show arrived.

A line of cars—odd makes and models—crept along Main Street in Reilly's Gulch traveling no faster than ten miles an hour. They'd come all the way from the airport at Great Falls at that excruciatingly slow pace.

Chester O'Reilly was in the lead in his bright-red Mazda Miata convertible, top down. The vehicles following him each had a hand-lettered placard taped to the windshield announcing it was part of O'Reilly's Taxi Service, no doubt the fastest growing business in the county. And they were all carrying out-of-towners holding hundred-dollar admission tickets to the Designs by Arletta show to be held that afternoon at the Cattlemen's Association.

Two hundred tickets at a lesser price had been reserved for local residents. The entire show was a sell-out despite the fact no one knew quite what to do with the lingering scent of steer manure in the building, deciding it was simply a part of the unique ambience.

Outside the building, two TV networks' remote vans were parked with their satellite dishes pointed upward. The weather report predicted a storm later in the week, but for now the day was a perfect one, the cloudless sky a Wedgwood blue.

Arletta was crazed, snipping and sewing last-minute alterations on her designs while the five models brought in from New York took the excitement in stride. Or perhaps they were exhausted from the raucous party they'd enjoyed last night at Sal's. Even more possibly, they were saving their energy for one last fling tonight with a determined group of cowboys.

Racing from one crisis to another, Tasha wondered why on earth anyone had thought she'd be able to organize an event this complicated. Or why in heaven's name she'd agreed to try.

One of the child models had run into a ladder, a makeshift stand for a spotlight, nearly bringing the light crashing to the floor and giving herself a bloody nose in the process. A couple of teachers and a PTA mom came to the rescue by giving first aid and corralling the children out of harm's way.

Tasha had sent Ella on an emergency trip to Great Falls when the printer's truck broke down and the programs weren't going to make it for show time.

In the past two weeks, she'd made a million phone calls from Cliff's house—most of them long distance—and she probably owed him her entire paycheck from the next modeling job she landed. Assuming she ever worked again in the business if Arletta's show flopped.

Someone's makeup kit had gone missing and Tasha sent Cliff racing to the house to bring back her own because none of the other girls had the right colors.

The guitar player's amplifier developed a short. Arnie, the owner of the local garage, jury-rigged a fix without electrocuting himself. Or burning down the building. Small blessing.

About the time Tasha thought nothing else could go wrong, a dog got loose inside the auditorium and chased a cat beneath the bunting that lined the runway, then dashed out an exit door that someone had left open.

"Oh, my God," she groaned, her head swimming. This couldn't be happening to her. She was a model; she put on the clothes, someone said she looked good and she walked out onto the runway and into the lights. Dogs, cats and assorted small children did not disrupt her performance.

Until now.

At the moment she thought she'd collapse, a strong arm circled her waist, keeping her upright. Gratefully, she inhaled Cliff's spicy scent and, despite her intentions not to rely on him, she leaned into his strength. Dressed in his uniform, he was acting as head of security for the event.

"Has anyone told you lately that you're terrific?" he asked.

Terrific in bed, but not necessarily all that swift organizing a fashion show.

"I can't remember," she mumbled.

"It's true. Things are going beautifully."

"Arletta's having a nervous breakdown. She ran out of navy-blue thread."

"Candy gave her some. Not to worry."

Candy? Aw, hell, why couldn't it have been Ella who saved the day.

"The show's about to start, honey. I gotta get back out front. I just wanted to wish you luck."

"Thanks," she murmured, still feeling frantic. She had no idea how the critics would view Arletta's designs. Or the show itself. She only knew enough tickets had been sold to make the show a success for the school district. Reilly's Gulch Elementary School would open in the fall. The school board president and Marc Toomey had assured her of that, given the gate receipts.

Tasha's only regret was that she wouldn't be in town to enjoy the celebration.

She was slipping into her outfit for the opening number—a winter silk skirt that showed a lot of leg and a clingy blouse—when Bobby Bruhn came sauntering into the dressing area.

His lips twisting into an approving smile, he looked her up and down. "Hmm, very nice. I should have volunteered my help hours ago."

"We're real busy here, Bobby." She snared her

heels and slid her feet into them. "No visitors are allowed backstage."

"I'm not visiting, sweetheart. I'm just looking for equal time."

Her hands froze at midzipper on her skirt and she raised her eyebrows.

"They said out front that you're in charge."

"I guess," she said cautiously.

His gaze traveled past her to one of the other models who was only half-dressed. "I'd like a chance to talk to the good folks of Reilly's Gulch about the election." Slowly he dragged his gaze back to Tasha. "Nothing long-winded, you understand. Just a little welcome to the show, thanks for supporting the school, vote for the best man—"

"Sorry, Bobby, this isn't a political event—"

"I'm only asking for equal time with what Cliff's getting—in the interest of political fairness, you understand."

"Cliff's handling security." She smoothed her hair and shot a quick look in a mirror hanging from a clothes rack.

In the auditorium, the combo hit a fanfare worthy of *Aida,* the models lined up for their first entrance, the children beside them wearing their brand-new outfits.

"Gotta go, Bobby."

Tasha found Melissa and Stevie and took their hands as Arletta announced with a flourish, "Welcome to Arletta's world!"

The models hit the runway at full stride to resounding applause. Tasha couldn't recall a fashion show that had received such a warm welcome. The enthusiasm of the moms and dads in the back rows spilled over onto the critics, who were all smiling. It didn't matter to anyone that Arletta's designs were eminently impractical to wear in this part of Montana. They were experiencing a *happening* that extended beyond normal boundaries of life, bringing people together.

Costume changes became a blur, models swiftly changing from one outfit to another as they had rehearsed that morning. The pace was fast, Arletta's introductory patter rapid-fire, the critics and retail buyers hard-pressed to keep up with their notes.

Soon everyone backstage was breathless, Tasha included. It was a chaos of dresses draped haphazardly over rods and half-naked women scurrying to clothe themselves before their next entrance.

The honor of wearing the final gown went to Tasha. Working quickly so she wouldn't be late for her cue, she slipped on the white wedding gown and pinned it at the shoulder with a gold clip. Far from traditionally styled, the long, form-fitting skirt had a slit up the side to allow for walking while showing off the length and shape of her legs.

Beside her, Melissa was dressed in a pink frilly dress and Stevie in a Western-Cut tuxedo with a red vest, formal attire junior-size.

The music segued into a slower number and she took their hands, stepping from behind the curtain onto the runway.

"Chins up, kids," she whispered. "And give 'em a big Montana smile."

The audience hushed. They knew this was the last of Arletta's designs, the grand finale, yet they were entirely quiet. For a moment, Tasha panicked. Had she forgotten to zip something? Smeared her makeup into a clown face? Beyond the footlights had the audience vanished, lifted skyward by Ricky Monroe's visiting space aliens?

Or had they decided to express their disapproval because of the election-motivated gossip about Tasha and Cliff?

Using every ounce of professionalism she possessed, she walked forward. Only then did she realize how she and the children appeared, and who was waiting for her at the other end of the runway.

Tasha stumbled, squeezing the children's hands more tightly. For a moment it seemed so real. A dream come true, a dream she hadn't dared allow herself. She was the bride in white, Melissa and Stevie her attendants, Cliff, her groom, smiling his sexy grin and wearing a tuxedo matching Stevie's.

Slowly the applause began, starting from the back of the room. Flashbulbs popped. Cameras whirred. And Cliff began striding down the runway toward her. He offered his arm.

"Hi, Daddy," Stevie said loudly enough for the audience to hear. "Did you see me modeling?"

"Sure did, bucko. You're looking good." He winked at Tasha as he took his son's place next to her, and her heart somersaulted in her chest.

"Me, too," Melissa insisted. "I'm real pretty. And so's my mommy."

"You got that straight, little Ms. Goldilocks. Prettiest bride Reilly's Gulch has ever seen. She takes my breath away.''

Tasha could barely breathe at all.

A ripple of approving laughter spread through the room.

''Whose idea was this?'' Tasha managed to ask as they paraded down the runway, realizing now this was what Bobby Bruhn was talking about. She kept her smile in place, but her heart was beating faster than any Texas two-step. This was only a fashion show. A fund-raiser. She wasn't getting married. That dream would never come true.

''Arletta asked for volunteers for the finale,'' Cliff said. ''As soon as I heard you were the bride, I couldn't let her pick anyone else for the groom, now could I?''

She let go of his arm, made a graceful turn at the end, pirouetting to let the audience get a good look at the designer gown, then faced him again. ''You could have told me.'' Her smiling lips never moved.

''And spoil the surprise? Not a chance.''

Another turn and a pose for more pictures, arms linked again, then a return to the start of the runway where the other models joined them for one last bow. The applause was thunderous. But Tasha's heart was breaking. Tomorrow she'd be leaving Reilly's Gulch. And Cliff.

TASHA INTENDED to change into street clothes, but she was mobbed by well-wishers before she could get away to the makeshift dressing room they'd curtained off from the public. In the confusion she lost track of Cliff and the children, but had faith that he was watching out for them. He was such a good father, caring and concerned about everything Stevie did. He was that way with Melissa, too.

"Spectacular job." Marc Toomey bent over her hand to give her a kiss. "I wasn't sure a small town like this could pull it off, but you did."

"I had a lot of help."

Arletta found her and gave her a quick hug before a New York newspaper critic drew her away for additional comments. Several buyers were lined up to give praise and place orders.

The school board president paid his respects as did all the other members with the exception of Winnie. Tasha wasn't sure she'd even been in the audience. She hadn't seen the preacher and his ladies, either. But then, it was hard to see beyond the footlights.

Several mothers approached her, all gushing about how much their children had enjoyed being models. Feeling like a piano teacher after a student recital, Tasha thanked them for their participation.

She'd let down her hair, slipped behind the dressing room curtain, at last able to draw a quick breath when a reporter with a TV cameraman in tow caught up with her. The young, attractive woman—who looked vaguely familiar—introduced herself as being from a major network news program doing human interest stories.

"We're doing a segment on small towns trying to save their schools. It's a problem all rural areas have and we think you've found a unique solution."

The woman signaled her cameraman, the lights went on and she stuck a microphone in Tasha's face. "How did you come up with the idea of a fashion show, Tasha?"

Tasha mentally stumbled over an answer. She hadn't meant to take the spotlight. But she could hardly refuse to answer the reporter's questions. If nothing else, being seen on national television would certainly help her career. And maybe she could help the town of Reilly's Gulch, too.

THE CROWD had dispersed and Ella had taken charge of Melissa and Stevie when Cliff spotted Tasha talking with the TV reporter. She looked tired, almost wan, but he hadn't lied about her taking his breath away when she'd appeared in that slinky, sexy wedding dress. Now she looked as if she needed rescuing. He was the man for the job.

He sauntered up to her, keeping just out of camera range. "Ms. Reynolds has an important phone call," he said to the reporter. "Are you about through?"

The reporter glanced at him, gave him a quick once-over, including a close scrutiny of his uniform that he'd changed back into, then smiled seductively. "Sure," she said, a trace of her New York accent apparent when the cameras weren't running. "I hear there's going be some party at a place called Sal's. You planning to be there?"

"Naw, my kids are sick with the croup and the old lady's down with female problems. Pregnant again, you know. This'll be number six. Or maybe seven. I forget." Cliff had come across cop groupies before. He wasn't interested, no matter how attractive they might be. "But maybe I can join you later. Where're you staying?"

The young woman blanched and waved to her cameraman. "That's a wrap, Speed. Let's get back to the shop."

Tasha waited until the reporter was out of hearing, then said, "*Six or seven?* And you can't *remember?*" Amusement danced in her bright blue eyes.

"You looked like you were ready to collapse."

"I still am. I can't ever remember being this stressed out before. As far as I'm concerned, that reporter can have all the fun at Sal's that she wants. I'm exhausted." She reached for the gold pin on her shoulder, her fingers trembling as she tried to unlatch it.

"Here, let me." He worked the clasp, her nearness and sultry scent making his fingers as clumsy as hers. "You wowed them, you know. Every guy in the audience fell a little bit in love with you." Cliff knew he'd fallen a *lot* in love with Tasha, but with people still milling around, taking down lights and packing up the chairs, this didn't seem like a good time to mention how he felt.

"As long as the school gets its money and Arletta gets good press for her designs, I'm happy."

She slid her dress off and reached for a lightweight robe hanging nearby. As Cliff held it for her to slip on, he was struck by a powerful punch of jealousy. If Tasha went back to New York, guys would be ogling her every day. Maybe some of them catching a glimpse of her half-dressed as he just had.

It didn't matter to her. This was her business. And she was sure wearing more than most women wore at the beach.

But it mattered to Cliff. He wanted to be the only man to see her any way but fully clothed.

He lifted her long hair free of the robe's collar and kissed her nape. "You've been avoiding me since we made love," he whispered. "Now that the show's over, I'm not going to let you get away with that anymore. Tonight's the night, sweetheart."

"Cliff—" Her voice caught on a husky note.

"I don't plan to take no for an answer. And I'm hoping the kids will go to bed real early."

Before Tasha had a chance to object, a couple of the models came by, full of effervescent enthusiasm about the show, and expressed their appreciation for being included. Right after that, one of the workmen from the rental company had a question for her.

Cliff stood by, watching. He'd bide his time for now. But tonight she'd be all his again. Then he'd tell her how he felt and, if he had his way, they'd start making plans to put that wedding gown to good use.

THE PHONE RANG so often during dinner, Tasha finally began taking the congratulatory calls in the spare room Cliff laughingly referred to as his office so the rest of them could eat in peace. She hadn't expected so much appreciation from people she barely knew. Some of them she hadn't actually met, yet still they'd made it a point to call. Though tired from all the advance planning and stress, her adrenaline continued to pump, keeping her on a mental high.

As she hung up from the most recent call, she leaned back in Cliff's desk chair and sighed. All this attention made her feel…as if she belonged, she realized. Suddenly she wasn't an outsider—a New Yorker on a brief holiday.

Suddenly everyone knew her and wanted to be her friend.

That astonishing realization set her back on her mental heels. Would it be possible for her and Melissa to make a new life here—with Cliff and his son?

"Oh, my…" she whispered. Did she dare consider that possibility?

Standing, she paced around the cluttered room. Cliff had a computer, which he rarely used. There were cardboard cartons stacked in one corner; a bookshelf lined the wall opposite the windows, a messy collection of books on both legal issues and raising cattle. Several rolls of blueprints were piled beside the bookcase. Idly she picked up one and unrolled it.

House plans, she concluded. She knew Cliff and his wife had had this house custom built. But if she was reading these plans correctly, they were for a two-story structure. Odd. Maybe they'd run out of money.

"You want me to save the rest of your dinner for you?" Cliff asked from the doorway. "The kids and I are about to clean up the kitchen."

She started. "No, that's all right. I'm too much on edge to eat anyway."

"I want you to keep up your strength for tonight, sweetheart. I plan to keep you awake for a long time."

Anticipation rippled through her. If only she could belong here...belong to Cliff. "In that case, maybe you'd better have a few extra calories yourself, cowboy. We New Yorkers are known for our endurance."

"We'll see about that, Ms. Goldilocks." He laughed, and his wicked smile nearly undid her right there in the middle of his office. Crossing the room, he took the blueprint from her. "What do you think?"

"I think you can be a very persuasive fellow."

"No, I meant about the house. We built the place originally with expansion in mind so there'd be plenty of room for the children."

"Children?"

He spread the blueprint out on top of the cluttered desk. "Yeah, I wasn't kidding about six or seven kids. Yvonne and I both wanted a large family, though we were willing to take them one kid at a time." Tilting his head, he studied the plans, a little smile playing at the corners of his lips. He pointed to a room outlined on the as-yet-uncompleted second floor. "That's the playroom. Winters are the pits here. We figured the kids would need someplace where they could stay out of our hair or none of us would survive the winter months."

Tasha's heart sank into her stomach. She couldn't

give him six or seven children. One—her beloved Melissa—was the only child she'd ever bear. "Why so many?" she asked, desperate for a reprieve, some reason why he might give up his dream of a big family.

"She was an only child and envied kids with lots of siblings." He rolled the blueprint again, searching across the top of his messy desk for a rubber band. "And I always wanted a big family, probably as a way to compensate for Bryant being my only blood relative."

So reasonable. So understandable. And yet so beyond her ability to give him what he desired.

The phone rang. Tasha nearly jumped out of her skin.

"It's probably for you," Cliff said. Leaning toward her, he brushed a quick kiss to her lips, a sensual promise of how he intended to spend the rest of the night. "Make it as quick as you can and we'll unplug the damn thing. I'll get the kids ready for bed."

Tasha's hand shook as she picked up the instrument. Her dreams, those she'd held so briefly, had just shattered. She couldn't shatter Cliff's dreams, too. He deserved to father all the children he wanted; he deserved a wife who could help him achieve his dream.

"Hello," she said into the phone after Cliff left to see to the children. Her throat ached as much as her heart.

"Tasha, my love, it's Peter Strauss."

The agent who'd turned down the chance to represent her. Why would he—

"You made the evening news, lovey. Great visibility. Perfect timing."

"Peter, I'm really pretty busy right now." And heartsick.

"Nolan Twardowski, the CEO of Nature's Hair Care spotted you, and he wants you, lovey. He and I have worked together before and he gave me a ring at home. He's putting an offer on the table for you to be Nature's Hair Care spokeswoman. A five-year contract at a minimum. I told him you wouldn't be able to resist."

Stunned, confused by a sea of emotions she couldn't control, Tasha barely had enough sense to ask questions about the deal. She wasn't thrilled to have Peter as her agent since he'd turned her down only weeks ago. But he was aggressive making deals for his clients, even though in this case the advertiser was a personal friend. And when she hung up, she knew it was a contract any woman in the world would be a fool not to sign. Her financial future and Melissa's would be secure.

But it didn't change the truth. She couldn't be the woman a man like Cliff deserved. Nor could a lucrative contract repair a heart that would never be whole again.

As she walked into the kitchen, she braced herself to break the news that she and Melissa would be leaving tomorrow as planned.

Chapter Eleven

Cliff had an assembly line going. Melissa brought him the dishes from the table, he rinsed them in the sink and Stevie put them in the dishwasher. Very efficient. Cliff had a vested interest in moving the kitchen cleanup along at warp speed tonight, he thought with a grin. That and getting the kids to bed on time.

He glanced over his shoulder when Tasha returned to the kitchen. Despite her solemn expression, his body responded in a basic, primal way he hoped the kids wouldn't notice. He suspected his reaction to Tasha would always be the same— heated and urgent.

"Time to pull the plug on the phone," he said, deciding he liked her as well in jeans as he did in the sexy dresses she'd worn for the fashion show. But naked and beneath him would be even more to his liking. "We've got better things to do with our time." Even to his own ears, his voice sounded husky. Suggestive.

Her expression remained unchanged, and Cliff got

a bad feeling right between his shoulder blades. "What's wrong?"

"That last call was from one of the agents I'd contacted a couple of weeks ago. He made me an offer I can't turn down."

If she'd punched him in the gut, the air couldn't have left Cliff's lungs any faster. "What kind of an offer?"

She gathered up the unused silverware from the table and put the utensils back in the drawer where they belonged. "A hair products company wants me to be their spokesperson. The CEO evidently saw me on the evening news and called the agent at home. It's a five-year contract with an option to renew. A very lucrative deal. More than I ever hoped for."

"Are you going to be on TV, Mommy?"

"Yes, dear. They'll be buying network time, a big promotional push." She cupped the back of her daughter's head, focusing on Melissa and no one else in the room. "And that means I need for you to check around the house this evening before bedtime and gather up all of your things. We'll pack in the morning, then leave for home."

Melissa's eyes turned as wide as blue saucers. "Home?"

"You're going back to New York." Cliff didn't need to ask the question; he already knew it was true. The sense of betrayal shot through him, sharp and deep. He'd wanted her to stay. She hadn't given him a chance to ask.

She nodded.

"I don't want to go home," Melissa complained.
"I like it here with Uncle Cliff."

"The job's in New York, honey. Taping will
start—"

"No! I'm not going!" Melissa's eyes flooded and
tears spilled down her cheeks, her chin quivering.
"You can't make me go!"

Stevie launched himself at Tasha and wrapped his
arms around her waist. "Don't make her go, Aunt
Tasha. Melissa's my *cousin!*" he wailed.

"If you need someone to baby-sit Stevie, I'm sure
Ella will be happy…" Her voice broke. "Your
housekeeper will be back soon."

"Uncle Cliff, *pleeease!*"

Cliff's gaze met Tasha's, and he saw regret in her
eyes. Or maybe he imagined the tears through the
sheen of his own.

"Kids! That's enough," he said sharply.

"No, I won't go—"

"Melissa can stay with me forever 'n ever—"

Kneeling beside his son, Cliff pried Stevie's arms
free of Tasha and hugged the boy. His own throat
hurt like hell, tears clogging it so full, he could
barely speak. "Your Aunt Tasha has to make the
decision that's right for her and Melissa."

"No, she doesn't," Stevie sobbed.

Tasha tried to talk to her daughter, but Melissa
would have none of it. She went racing from the
room, her feet pounding on the hardwood floor.

"Make her stay," Stevie pleaded. "Please,
Daddy."

He glanced up at Tasha. Afraid to ask; afraid not

to. In front of his son, he was unable to express all he felt, all he wanted. "If I asked you to stay, would you?"

She'd gone pale. Her throat worked, but otherwise she had no more animation than a department store mannequin. "I can't," she whispered.

Why the hell not? he wanted to ask. But a man had to keep some part of his pride. Cliff remembered after his mother had abandoned him and Bryant at the church, a police officer kept saying, "Don't cry, boys. You're gonna be fine. You're big boys, aren't you? Big boys don't cry."

Cliff had tried so hard not to cry then. He was trying just as hard now. The sense of abandonment was just as painful. Just as hopeless.

"Come on, son. Let's help Melissa get her things together."

HOURS LATER when the house was quiet, Tasha took the remaining blouse from its hanger in the closet, folded it carefully and laid it in her suitcase.

This was the hardest thing she'd ever had to do. She directed all her energy at holding herself together. Of not letting go and telling Cliff the real reason she was leaving.

Damaged goods. That was what her husband had called her following the surgery to remove a tumor…and her uterus. And when he'd left her only months later "to find himself," he'd made it clear that no man worth his salt would ever want her. *Not a skinny, empty shell of a woman.*

The hurt and shame she'd felt six years ago knifed

through her again just as sharply as the scalpel they'd used then. She'd never told anyone. Not even her family. She hadn't wanted their pity. Nor had she wanted to see the truth in their eyes. *Only half a woman.*

Taking her undies from the drawer, she told herself she was doing the right thing for both herself and her daughter. And for Cliff and his son.

Melissa's tears had nearly undone her. But the child was resilient. At heart, she loved New York. Loved being pampered by her grandparents who lived nearby. With the irrepressible spirit of youth, she'd quickly adjust to being back home.

Meanwhile, Tasha was leaving her heart here in Montana. It wouldn't do her any good in New York. The pieces were already shattered beyond repair.

When she finished packing, she put on her nightgown and crawled under the covers. But she knew sleep would elude her. Only hours ago Cliff had made a sensual promise to keep her awake by making love to her the whole night—or as long as her strength held out. Did she have the right to ask him to fulfill that promise even though she'd be leaving in the morning?

She covered her mouth with her hand, stifling a sob. Selfishly, she wanted that memory to take back with her to New York. Their last night together.

Slipping out of bed, she walked barefoot from her room across the hallway to Cliff's door. The house was country-quiet, a stillness that was almost physical and pressed in on her ears, making her aware of the blood pulsing through her veins. She placed her hand on the doorknob; the latch clicked as she turned it and she swung the door open.

"Cliff, are you awake?" she whispered.

"Yeah, I'm awake. What do you want?" He didn't sound particularly happy about her unexpected arrival.

She closed and locked the door behind her, praying he wouldn't reject her, then made her way to his bed. She sat down beside him.

Cliff's body tensed. He swallowed hard. "What is this? Some kind of a charitable fond farewell?"

"What does it matter as long as we both want it?"

He wanted to send her away. If nothing else, he wanted to prove he had some small bit of pride left. But then she bent over him, her long, silky hair caressing his bare chest, and she kissed him. Instantly he was lost in her taste, her scent, the feel of her body sliding down beside him on the bed.

With an anguished sound of frustration, he surrendered to her. Surrendered to his need. To the ache that had been building for the past two weeks. Or maybe the past three years. She was here now. Ready to ease his pain. He could not refuse her. Or himself.

He rose on one elbow and kissed her. Just kissed her. Slowly delving his tongue inside. Making it last. Tasting her as he would savor a peach freshly picked from a tree on a hot summer day, juicy and sweet.

Her breathing became ragged. So did his. And still he kissed her, skimming her beautifully shaped brows with his lips, toying at the sensitive spot beneath her ear. Returning to her mouth again and again.

She squirmed beside him. "Cliff…"

"Not yet."

She moaned a low, throaty sound, her fingers digging into his back. "Please…"

"Remember, this was your idea. That means I get to set the pace."

"No," she protested. "I want—"

He cupped her breast through the fabric of her gown, flicking his thumb over the already taut nipple.

"Yes," she sighed. "Kiss me there. Everywhere."

He planned to do as she wanted, but he was still going to take his time. She wouldn't forget this night. Neither would he.

With infinite patience, he edged her nightgown up above her hips. He kissed her belly, then lifted the gown higher, venturing farther, laving first one breast then the other. When she was trembling, he shifted his attentions lower, tempting but not giving her what she wanted.

She writhed, twisted and turned, she lifted her hips, frantic to get closer, but he wouldn't let her. Not yet. Not until neither of them could endure another moment of this sweet torment.

"Torture," she sobbed.

"Yes," he agreed. His jaw ached from clenching his teeth.

He'd never experienced such pleasure as he did now, lengthening the moment, holding off the ultimate intimacy until he knew they were both on the brink. She was bare to him, her body slick with sweat. So was his when he finally eased her legs apart and entered her in one swift stroke.

She shattered around him, pumping hard, crying out, and he began to count backward from a hundred in a monumental effort to control his own release.

Only when her breathing had returned to near normal did he begin again. Stroking rhythmically. Feeling her liquid heat.

Her fingers combed through his hair, bringing his mouth to hers. Her hips rose to meet his, faster and faster, fighting to prevent him from pulling away. He sank back inside her only to withdraw again.

"Now," she cried, her eager hips coming up off the bed to tempt him back again.

"Yes, now." He thrust deeply, no longer able to control himself. His release came with the power of a geyser, nature's explosive force. He buried his face at the crook of her neck, muffling his cry as best he could as his body continued to pulse into her.

From the depth of his soul, he knew this woman was his. And still she planned to leave him. The unfairness of life left him weak with pain and disappointment.

TASHA WOKE LATE the next morning to the knowledge Cliff no longer shared the bed and that this was the day she'd be leaving Montana. Despite the late hour, scant light crept into the room through the curtained window. Outside, rain dripped from the eaves like the tears that clogged Tasha's throat.

Weary in both body and soul, she threw back the covers and got out of bed. She was doing the right thing. In time Cliff would find someone else; he'd fill all those bedrooms with the children he so richly deserved.

But they wouldn't be *her* children. That realization nearly drove her to her knees.

The house seemed oddly quiet as she went across the hall to her room, the overcast sky turning everything gray both inside and outside the house. She showered and dressed in her traveling clothes, slacks and a comfortable blouse. Her bag was packed, on the bed ready to close.

She found Cliff at the kitchen table drinking coffee and looking as morose as she felt. His work shirt hung open, the sleeves rolled up. His hair was mussed as though he hadn't combed it yet.

She edged past him to get coffee for herself. "Where are the children?"

He shrugged. "Still sleeping, I guess."

Frowning, she poured coffee into a mug. Usually the children were up by now, filling the air with giggles or childish arguments. Last night they'd been upset by her announcement that she and Melissa would be leaving this morning.

A prickle of unease slid down her spine. She set her mug on the counter. "I think I'll check...."

Keeping her imagination under control, she hurried down the hallway. There was no reason to panic. The door to the children's room was closed. She shoved it open, her palm slick with sweat on the doorknob, her stomach churning with anxiety.

In the dusky gloom she could make out a lumpy form under the covers on both beds. The children were still sleeping. Relieved, she smiled at her unfounded case of the jitters. Talk about an overprotective mother!

She walked around Stevie's bed to get to her daughter's to wake her. They had a long journey in front of them and first they'd have to stop at the Double S to say goodbye to Ella and the baby.

Placing her hand on the lumpy form under the covers, she immediately knew something was wrong. She yanked back the blankets only to discover a pillow and stuffed animals hidden there. No Melissa.

Whirling, wings of panic rising like the winds of a hurricane, she stripped the blankets away from Stevie's bed. He was gone, too.

"Cliff!" she screamed. "The children!"

Tasha's bloodcurdling scream shot Cliff out of his chair as if he'd been launched by a rocket. He raced to the back of the house, halting abruptly at the door to Stevie's bedroom. Tasha's eyes were rounded with fear, her complexion pale.

"What's wrong?"

Her chin trembled. "The children. They're gone."

Cliff did a quick scan of the room, noting the pile of pillows on both beds. "They're probably playing a trick on us." He looked under the bed. Nothing. In two strides he was at the closet, yanking the door open, peering behind the clothes, expecting to hear childish giggles giving away the game. "Hide-'n-seek, that's what they're up to."

"I think they've run away."

"No. Stevie wouldn't do that." He checked the overflowing toy box. His son wouldn't go off and leave him. They were too close; they'd been through too much together. "They're probably hiding out in the barn. I'll check." Striding out of the room, he buttoned his shirt and started to tuck his shirt in his jeans.

Tasha was right behind him. "I'm coming with you."

"It's raining."

"I've been wet before."

He grabbed his jacket and Stetson on the way out the back door. Tasha didn't bother with a coat for herself. Cliff didn't say anything. They'd find the kids in the barn, give 'em a good talking to for scaring the daylights out of them, and Tasha could dry out before she and Melissa left.

Left. God, he could still barely believe Tasha was leaving him. Little wonder the kids were upset. Cliff felt like doing something extreme himself.

The temperature had dropped twenty degrees from what it had been yesterday. The rain that had started in the night had soaked into the ground, leaving shallow puddles between the house and the barn. Unconcerned, Cliff marched through them. He hadn't been out to check on the horses yet this morning. Maybe Stevie had taken care of that for him.

Shoving open the barn door, he stepped inside,

the air warmer and ripe with the scent of hay and animals. Sunny Boy nickered in greeting and shook his head. Henry pawed the ground in his stall at the far end of the barn, snorting softly.

But to Cliff's dismay, the other stalls were empty. Star Song and Peaches were gone, their stalls standing open, the horses' saddles missing from the rack.

Cliff cursed.

"They've run away, haven't they?" Worry and fear laced Tasha's voice, making it quaver. "And taken the horses."

"Looks like it." He headed for the tack room to see what else the children might have taken, how well equipped they might be.

"It's my fault. Melissa was so upset about leaving—"

"Nobody's to blame. They're kids. Kids don't always understand." In this case, neither did Cliff. He wanted Tasha to stay, but he wouldn't ask. She had a career to pursue. That was what she'd wanted all along. Never once had she said otherwise. Ironing his shirts wasn't her bag.

"What if they're lost out there somewhere. Or a horse throws them. It's cold and rainy. Anything could happen. A horse could slip...."

"They're probably only going as far as Bryant's place. Stevie knows the way." Except Cliff discovered a couple of sleeping bags were missing from the shelf in the tack room. Saddle bags, too. If they were only running away as far as the main ranch, they wouldn't have needed those items. But he was going to keep that information to himself for now.

He wasn't ready to frighten Tasha any more than she already was. "Let's go back inside and I'll call Bryant, tell him to keep an eye out for the kids."

"Shouldn't we go after them?"

"We don't know how long ago they left. They could already be at Bryant's by now."

She hurried to keep pace with him. "They'll be all right, won't they?"

"They'll be fine." Once back in the house, he went straight to his office. "While I'm calling Bryant, why don't you see what kind of clothes they took with them? Jackets and rain gear?"

She vanished down the hallway and Cliff dialed Bryant's number. His brother answered the phone.

"Hey, Bry, we've got a little problem over here."

"Yeah? What's that?" Bryant sounded relaxed. In the background, Jason was making happy baby noises. Cliff squelched a surge of envy. Bryant deserved all the happiness he could get. They both did.

Too agitated to sit down, Cliff paced around the desk as far as the phone cord would allow. "Looks like Stevie and Melissa have run away from home. I thought they might have shown up at your place."

There was a long pause on the other end of the line. "I haven't seen 'em yet. How long ago did they leave?"

"We don't exactly know."

"Should I ask why they'd want to run away?"

"Tasha's got a job lined up in New York. She's...she was planning to leave this morning."

"I'm sorry, Bro. I thought maybe the two of you—"

"Yeah, well, I kinda thought so, too." He looked up as Tasha came back into the room. Rain had stained her blouse dark across her shoulders and loosened her hair, causing strands to curl along the column of her neck. Watching Cliff on the phone, she hugged herself, her expression a combination of misery and fear. "Keep an eye out for the kids, okay?" Cliff told his brother.

"Will do. I'll send Rusty and the boys out looking. Try not to worry. We'll find 'em."

"Right. Thanks, Bry." Cliff cradled the phone.

"No sign of them?" Tasha asked.

"Not yet."

"They're wearing their jackets. That's something."

"Yeah. Something." And the fact that it wasn't likely to snow was good, too. But the early June rain was cold. It didn't have to be below freezing for a kid to suffer from hypothermia, particularly if he got soaked through to the skin.

"And it looks like they took a loaf of bread and the jar of peanut butter from the pantry. So they aren't hungry."

"That's good. Sounds like they did some planning ahead."

She placed her hand on her chest as if she were having trouble breathing. "I feel so guilty. Last night while we were making love, the children were—" Her voice caught. Tears sheened her eyes. "And now—"

"Shh. Don't fall apart on me, honey." Crossing the room, he pulled Tasha into his arms. She trembled as he held her close. "We're in this together. We'll find 'em."

"She's my baby." She buried her face at the crook of his neck, stifling a sob.

"I know, sweetheart. I know." He felt the same way about Stevie. His son was his life, his heart. "Look, I'm going to call the sheriff. Maybe Larry can get a search party out here and a helicopter. They could cover a lot more ground than I can alone."

Drawing strength from somewhere deep inside herself, Tasha stepped away. "While you call the sheriff, I'll fix a thermos of coffee and some sandwiches. No telling how long it will take to find them."

Leaving Cliff to phone the sheriff, she went to the kitchen. Her knees felt weak, her chest ached. Dear heaven, what would she do if she lost Melissa? Her precious baby. The only child she'd ever have. Her womb felt more empty, more hollow that it ever had before.

With shaking hands, she slapped together bologna sandwiches, tossed a couple of apples into a sack along with some granola bars. Not that she expected to be hungry anytime soon. Her stomach was already lodged in her throat. She wouldn't be able to swallow a bite of food until they found Melissa and had her safely home again. And Stevie, too.

Several minutes had passed when the phone rang. Tasha held her breath. Surely that was Bryant calling to say the children had arrived at the

Double S. Or maybe some other neighbor had found them straying too far from home.

Cliff appeared in the doorway, his expression grim. "That was Bryant on the phone. When he and Rusty went out looking for the kids, they discovered about thirty steers are missing from the west section. A fence is down and there's evidence of an eighteen-wheeler going through the pasture."

"The rustlers?"

"Looks like." He walked past her to the locked cabinet where he kept his guns. "Meanwhile, the sheriff's rounding up some volunteers to help with the search, but the helicopter's a no-go. The ceiling's too low. This storm's going to get worse before it gets better."

"Dear God...our babies..."

He checked his handgun, slid it into a holster that he'd already strapped around his waist and took a rifle from the rack. He picked up two boxes of ammunition, which he dropped into his jacket pocket.

"I'm going to try to track the kids," he said. "If they didn't head for the main ranch, I think I know where else they might go."

"Where?"

"A line camp north of here. My dad built it for fishing trips on the river. I'll let you know what's happening as soon as I can."

"I'm going with you."

He shot her a startled look. "You can't. The terrain's too rough to take the truck, and I can track better if I'm mounted anyway."

She planted her fist on her hip. "I'm not going to

stay here chewing on my fingernails not knowing what's happening.''

"I've only got one horse left. Sunny Boy. You can't ride—"

"I'll ride the mule."

He gaped at her. "Don't be ridiculous. If nothing else, you'll slow me down. I won't have time to—"

"Just saddle the damn mule, Clifford. I swear to God, I won't slow you down, and if you don't let me come with you, I'll follow you one way or another. I won't leave my baby out there alone in the rain when there are rustlers around who could harm her.''

Pivoting on her heel, she went to the bedroom to get her jacket and rain slicker. She'd ride that damn mule to hell and back if she had to. She'd do anything to save her baby.

Chapter Twelve

Six hours later, Cliff reined his horse toward a stand of pines that would provide some protection from the wind and rain. He glanced over his shoulder at Tasha. He'd never met a more courageous woman. She'd been terrified of riding the mule. He'd seen it in her eyes and in the way her hands trembled. But she'd mounted Henry and had doggedly followed Cliff out of the corral, across the rolling prairie, down steep draws and up the other side without so much as a whimper. And now her hands had turned blue with cold.

So had Cliff's, for that matter, and he was wearing gloves. He cursed himself for not having thought to get her a pair, too.

He slowed beneath some trees out of the worst of the storm so Tasha could catch up with him. "We're going to stop here for the night."

Her head came up. The hood on her rain slicker dripped rain down her face, but it didn't erase the lines of fatigue around her eyes or the grim set of her lips. "We can't. The children—"

"I've lost the trail, Tasha. The rain has washed out the signs. It's no good to keep going in circles."

"C-circles?"

"Yeah. Didn't you notice?"

"No, I..." She lowered her head and her whole body shuddered.

Cliff dismounted and grasped Henry's bridle to steady the mule. "Off you come. We have to get you warmed up."

Except for her teeth chattering, she sat immobile in the saddle. "I c...can't move."

Worried about hypothermia, he let Sunny Boy's reins drop to the ground and looped his arm around Tasha's waist. "It's okay, honey. Let go of the reins and take your feet out of the stirrups, then lean toward me. I'll get you."

She managed to get her hands on his shoulders. He pulled her out of the saddle. When her feet touched the ground, her legs buckled. Cliff caught her.

"Easy does it, sweetheart," he murmured as she slumped against him.

"I'm s-sorry. I p-promised I wouldn't slow you down. And now..."

"It's the rain's fault, not yours. Come on." Half carrying her, Cliff got her under the shelter of a tree and eased her to the ground, where she moaned softly. "Hang on a minute while I get the animals settled and the tent up. Then we'll get you warm in the bedroll."

"I'm so worried about—"

"I know." So was Cliff, worried sick about the

kids, wondering if Stevie knew how to get in out of the storm, if the children were safe somewhere in their bedrolls. If they were as scared as Cliff was.

He hobbled Sunny Boy and the mule a distance from Tasha where the animals could find some grass to graze, then unsaddled them.

The tent he'd brought was little more than a tube of silk parachute fabric, but it would keep him and Tasha out of the wind and rain. He threaded a rope through the tent loops and strung it between a couple of trees, pulling the line taut. He tossed their two bedrolls inside, crawled in after them and zipped them together. He stashed his rifle and scabbard to one side of the tent.

''Okay.'' He pulled Tasha to her feet. Shaking, she stumbled against him. ''Into the tent you go and take off your clothes.''

''My clothes? I'll f-freeze.''

''That's what you're doing already. We're going to warm each other up the old-fashioned way.'' Later he'd make a small fire, but first he had to get Tasha's body temperature back to normal. The best way to do that was to cuddle.

While Tasha was undressing, Cliff got the saddlebags and thermos. The coffee would only be lukewarm by now, but it would help to heat their insides, and food would provide more fuel for their bodies.

When he returned, he got a quick glimpse of Tasha wearing only her lacy bra and underpants as she slipped inside the bedroll. Her skin was blue tinged and covered with goose bumps. He poured her some coffee.

"Here, drink this."

Her hands shook as she took the cup. "I've never been so c-cold." She drank half and handed the cup back to him. "You, too."

Gratefully he downed the remaining contents while she huddled down inside the bedroll and pulled it up over her shoulders. He gave her a half sandwich, which she ate with little enthusiasm.

He made quick work of undressing down to his shorts and T-shirt, then slid in beside her. He pulled her tight against his body and it was like embracing an iceberg.

"God, you should have told me how cold you were. We would have stopped sooner."

"I didn't want to stop. I thought we'd reach the fishing cabin and find them—"

"They turned off the trail a while back. I don't know if Stevie was confused or if he changed his mind about where he wanted to go." His son was only five years old. How could Cliff expect the boy to know his way around the Double S, a ten-thousand acre spread? With the cloud cover so low, even he had trouble keeping his bearings. And now they'd traveled almost to the Monroe land that butted against the west side of the Double S. Cliff and Bryant hadn't gone this far on their own until they were teenagers.

Tasha lay quietly in his arms, her shivers slowly subsiding. Another time, another place, Cliff would have been thinking about making love to her. But the intimacy they were sharing now was different than mere sexual passion, somehow deeper because it was based on their mutual fear for their children. Despite the burden of protecting Tasha, who admittedly wasn't used to the rigors of Montana, he was glad he wasn't facing this ordeal alone.

"Cliff, they could die out here, couldn't they?" Her pained whisper filled Cliff with the dread he didn't want to acknowledge.

"Don't even think that, honey. We'll find them."

"But how? We're stuck in this tent—"

"By now there are other search parties out looking for them. When the rain lets up, a helicopter and probably search-and-rescue planes will get into the act. Someone will find them."

"Please, God…"

Wind sighed through the trees like a prayer and rain dripped from the branches, plopping onto the nylon tent. The ground was hard and uneven. Spooned against him, Tasha pillowed her head on Cliff's shoulder, cherishing the feel of his body warming her flesh. Desperately, she tried not to think of what might be happening to Melissa. And Stevie. If she did, she'd go crazy with their inaction. Surely Cliff was right. Someone might have already found the children.

As her body warmed up, her mind drifted.

"You're going to miss a big candidate's meeting tonight," she said idly. "The last one before the election Tuesday."

"At the moment the election doesn't seem real important."

"Bruhn will be there. He'll probably turn your absence against you."

"It doesn't matter."

She smiled to herself. Tasha had known a lot of ambitious men, but few who'd willingly sacrifice their goals in order to search for two lost little children. Cliff had his priorities straight. His son ought to come first, just as Melissa was the most important person in Tasha's life and always would be.

But she'd discovered there was room in her heart for more than her only child. She loved Cliff and Stevie, too. Cliff had a right to know why she couldn't stay in Montana, why she couldn't tell him how much she loved him.

"I can't have any more children," she said softly.

For a moment he was so quiet, she wondered if he'd heard her. "You can't?"

She squeezed her eyes tightly shut against the dismay, the shock she heard in his voice. She swallowed the tears that filled her throat. "Shortly after Melissa was born I had a hysterectomy."

"Why? What went wrong?"

"A tumor. It was benign, but they still had to remove my uterus. They left my ovaries, which means I get to experience all the usual female mood swings without being able to have a child."

"God, I'm sorry, Tasha."

"The irony is that if I hadn't accidentally gotten pregnant when I did, I probably never would have been able to have children at all."

"A blessing in disguise."

She nodded, but her heart was breaking. Cliff

knew the truth now. Any moment he'd pull away from her—*half a woman, an empty shell*. Not a woman who could give him all the children he wanted and deserved.

But he continued to hold her and that shattered her heart into even smaller pieces. He was such a good man....

THE RAIN had slowed to only an occasional drop when Cliff stirred himself. In spite of his fears for Stevie, he could only hold a half-naked woman in his arms so long before biology took over. After Tasha had told him about her hysterectomy, he hadn't known what to say.

Hell, he was a guy. He had no idea how it felt to experience something like that. He didn't even know if she needed consoling, much less how to go about it.

She was a heck of a good mother, that much was clear. If it hadn't been for her surgery—and if she'd had a decent husband—she probably would have had a couple of kids by now. Maybe more.

Edging out of the bedroll, he put on his shirt and found his jeans, which were still damp, and pulled them on.

"I'm going to check on the weather," he said, tugging on his boots. "Maybe the sky's cleared some."

"I'll get dressed, too."

On all fours, he crawled out of the tent. The clouds had lifted, but the light was still muted, as much by the setting sun as by the cloud cover. First he went to check on his horse and the mule. They hadn't wandered far.

He was standing in the chill air giving Sunny Boy a good scratch between the ears when he heard a familiar sound. He froze.

In the woods sounds had a way of becoming distorted. You couldn't always tell the direction they came from or what you were hearing. Your own imagination—what you *wanted* to hear—could deceive you. Mislead you.

Cliff held his breath, listening so hard his ears ached with the effort.

A child's voice. Indistinct. In the distance. But definitely a child and one who sounded a lot like his son.

Cliff's heart rate accelerated. He raced to the tent and drew back the flap. "I hear them."

"What?"

"Stevie and Melissa. I can hear their voices."

She scrambled around to tug on her boots. "Where?"

"I'm not sure. But they've got to be close." So close that if he'd searched a little bit longer, he might have found the children already. Or maybe in the storm he would have gone past them, he reminded himself.

Extending his hand, he helped Tasha to her feet, strapped on his handgun and picked up his rifle. Then he led her to the horses and the rise where he'd heard the voices. He stood quietly for a moment, the rifle tucked under his arm, hearing only Sunny Boy munching on a clump of grass and a distant bird call. He knew this general area, although not well. He recalled the Monroes had a line camp somewhere nearby that Stevie had visited once with his buddy, Ricky. It was a small, rustic cabin much like the one the Swains had on a river north of here. He should have thought of it earlier and headed there to get out of the storm.

The sound came again, this time followed by a male voice. An *angry* male voice.

"There! I hear them!" Tasha cried. She cupped her mouth with her hands as though she were going to call out to the children. Cliff caught her arm, all of his law enforcement instincts on full alert. Puzzle pieces slid into place. "Don't. We don't know their situation."

Her perplexed frown tugged her brows together. "What are you talking about, their situation? I can hear Stevie—"

"There's an old cabin over that next rise and a dirt road. A road wide enough to handle an eighteen-wheeler if someone wanted to hide it in a remote area." His gut clenched. "I think our kids may have stumbled on the rustlers' hideout. Or Ricky Monroe's space aliens."

Tasha gasped. "No."

"You stay here while I—"

"We've come this far together. I'm not quitting now."

He eyed her cautiously. Despite her striking beauty and total femininity, Tasha was not the kind of woman who panicked easily. "It could be dangerous."

"All the more reason why you shouldn't go alone."

"Can you use a gun?"

Her jaw visibly tightened. "I can if I have to."

Cliff didn't want to create a situation where the kids would be in the line of fire. Nor did he want to put Tasha at risk. But going into an unknown situation without some sort of backup would be foolish on his part.

"Let's take this slowly until I can assess the situation. Stay well behind me. If we run into trouble, I want you to hightail it out of here and go for help. Got that?"

She nodded, but Cliff wasn't sure Tasha would do as she'd been told if she was forced to choose between escaping on her own or saving her child. It was a decision he hoped neither of them would have to make. Fortunately, thus far the rustlers hadn't used any weapons while committing their crimes. But when backed into a corner, criminals were unpredictable.

He checked his handgun, holstered it and turned to leave.

Tasha touched his arm, drawing him back. "Be careful," she whispered. "A dead hero won't do the children any good."

Leaning toward her, Cliff brushed a quick kiss to her lips. "Or a dead *heroine,*" he emphasized.

The wooded area where they'd camped was second growth, the pines maybe thirty feet tall and varied distances apart over a rolling landscape. Cliff kept clear of open areas as he moved stealthily over the rise and down the next hill. Behind him, Tasha stepped on a branch, snapping it. From somewhere ahead of him, childish voices continued to drift through the woods. A gruff male responded.

Dear God, he'd been raising his son in Montana thinking the boy would be safe from criminals. Now Stevie had walked right into their lair.

Cliff's heart pumped hard; adrenaline flooded his system. He called on all his years of training to do this one job right—to rescue his son and Tasha's daughter.

At the road he paused. Tire tracks had dug deep ruts. With little effort he spotted the telltale groove left by a rear tire, identifying the vehicle as the one belonging to the rustlers.

A little farther he spotted the cabin. A tiny wisp of smoke drifted out of the chimney. In a small corral nearby, Peaches and Star Song along with three other horses munched contentedly on hay that had been scattered in a feeding trough. If Cliff hadn't known better, the scene would appear tranquil.

But he'd learned through his police work that appearances could be deceiving.

He crouched down at the side of the trail and signaled Tasha to stop where she was and wait. He didn't know how many people might be in the cabin. He needed to get closer and he was going in alone.

TASHA HELD her breath as Cliff crept forward toward the small, wooden building. Every impulse she possessed demanded that she run past him, throw open the door of the cabin and take the children into her arms. She loved them both so much. She'd willingly use her own body to shield them from harm.

Yet surely Cliff knew what he was doing.

He vanished behind some trees and the minutes ticked by with such slowness, Tasha thought she'd go crazy waiting. Her mind was a jumble of thoughts and fears—her love for the children, her fear that Cliff would be killed. Her prayer that God wouldn't be that cruel, to take the man she'd come to love so deeply.

Suddenly, as silently as a breath of wind high in the trees, Cliff appeared beside her.

Without thinking, she threw herself into his arms, clinging to him, absorbing his strength, relishing the feel of his strong arms holding her. He'd make sure the children were safe. That was the kind of man he was.

She drew a steadying breath and pulled herself together. She couldn't be a burden to him, not now when the children were depending on him.

He cupped her cheek with his hand, using his thumb to wipe away tears she hadn't been aware she'd shed.

"There's only one man inside the cabin," he said. "I'd guess the rest of the rustlers left him behind to care for the horses. The kids seem to be arguing with him because he won't let them go."

"You've seen them?"

"Through the window. As nearly as I can tell, he hasn't harmed them. If anything, I suspect they're wearing the guy down."

Tasha couldn't conjure an ounce of sympathy for

the stranger who held her children captive. With a start, she realized she had "adopted" Stevie as her own—in her heart, if not in fact.

"Let's go get them." She stood.

He dragged her back down. "I don't know if he's armed, or if he intends to use the kids as hostages. What I need is a diversion to get him outside the cabin where I can get to him one-on-one."

"What can I do?"

"Not you. I'm going to get Henry down here, give him a swat and send him down the road to the cabin. With any luck he'll create enough of a ruckus that the guy inside will come out."

"Henry isn't exactly a predictable animal," she pointed out. "Likely as not, he'll take off in the opposite direction."

"It's still worth a shot."

"No. It'd be better if I rode him right up to the cabin and played the damsel in distress. Whoever is inside won't be able to resist finding out what's going on. And they won't suspect for a minute a mere woman has come to rescue the children."

"I can't let you—"

"There are two people in there whom I love, Clifford. Tell me my plan isn't better than just counting on Henry not to be ornery and go the wrong way, then I won't interfere. But you know my idea is a good one."

Cliff sat back on his haunches. He knew she was right. But he hated like hell to put a civilian at risk— to put *Tasha* at risk. Still, it was his son's life at stake as well as Tasha's daughter. They all deserved the best shot at a safe rescue.

Together they crept back up the hill to where the animals were grazing. Cliff saddled Henry.

"You sure you can do this?" he asked Tasha. "Henry can be pretty hard to handle."

"So can guys on the subway who want to cop a feel. Henry and I are going to reach an understanding in a hurry if he decides to act up this time."

She said it so seriously, with such a determined glint in her eyes, Cliff had to smile. Tasha Papadakis Reynolds was not a woman to be crossed when she got her dander up. If she ever married again, Cliff hoped her husband would understand that...and value the trait as much as he did.

"Okay," he said. "Give me a couple of minutes to get in position. Then you mount up and come down that road in front of the cabin making all the noise and confusion you can. With any luck at all, the man inside will leave the kids there and come out to see what's going on."

Her hand firmly gripping the bridle, she nodded.

"Good for you, sweetheart," he said and kissed her. With a stride as determined as Tasha's spirit, he headed off over the rise.

CLIFF DIDN'T waste time getting into position. It was getting darker by the minute and clouds were building again in the northwest, more stormy weather rolling in this direction. If he didn't secure the children's safety soon, he'd be at a disadvantage. He'd cleared the rise behind the cabin and hunkered down in sight of the front door just as he heard a blood-curdling scream. His head whipped toward the sound.

Henry trotted full tilt down the road at a gait that had Tasha bouncing out of the saddle with every step. Her feet had lost their purchase in the stirrups and her legs were flying wildly while she clung frantically to the saddle horn. She looked for all the world like a rag doll on a runaway mule. Which Cliff guessed was closer to the truth than Tasha might like.

"Help!" she screamed. Her hair had come loose and streamed down her back as though she were imitating a Nordic warrior woman. "Somebody help me!"

Pride and love filled Cliff's chest. What a woman!

She pounded past his hiding spot heading right for the cabin. "Help! I can't stop him! Some-body—"

The cabin door opened. A large man stepped out onto the porch. He wore a black T-shirt, old jeans, scruffy boots and looked vaguely familiar, someone Cliff had seen around town. He might be a hired hand on a local ranch or someone who hung out at Sal's and had gotten into a fight Cliff had to break up. Holding his breath, he waited for the stranger to step far enough away from the door so he couldn't duck back inside. From this angle, it didn't look as if the man was armed.

Tasha screamed again and somehow managed to aim Henry back toward the cabin, heading right for the stranger.

"Hey, lady. Pull up on the reins." Apparently unable to resist rescuing a beautiful woman, the man stepped off the porch.

Pistol drawn, Cliff made his move. In a few strides, he was at the side of the cabin. He shouted, "Police! You're under arrest. Get your hands up and get down on your knees. Now, mister!"

The guy cursed as Henry rocketed by, nearly knocking him over.

"Down!" Cliff warned again, afraid Tasha was taking too many risks.

The rustler sank to his knees, locking his hands behind his head as though he'd been this route before. Cliff would bet his badge the man had an arrest record.

"Daddy! Daddy!" Stevie burst out the door.

"Stay back, son." Cliff approached his prisoner cautiously. "Is there anyone else inside the cabin?"

"Only Melissa." Stevie halted at the edge of the porch. "I told that man you were a deputy, that you'd come find us and 'rest him, but he didn't believe me."

Melissa shot out of the cabin onto the porch. "He's a bad man, Uncle Cliff. You gotta take him to jail."

"That's just what I intend to do." Still holding his gun on the rustler, Cliff did a quick frisk of the man without finding any weapons, all the time wondering what had happened to Tasha. She'd disappeared into the woods and he could hear the harsh snap of branches marking her trail.

The rustler cursed again. "I told Bobby we was gonna get caught."

Cliff hesitated. "Bobby?" His mind raced. It couldn't be, yet there was a certain logic to— "You're talking about Bobby Bruhn?"

"Hell, yeah. He thinks he's the brains behind all this rustling, but he's a damned idiot. No way are they gonna elect him sheriff of squat."

"Why would he even want to be sheriff?"

"'Cause then we could make off with all the beef we wanted and who's to know. He sure as hell wouldn't be arresting anybody, not when he was behind it all."

Rain began to spatter on the ground again, but Cliff ignored it. He had some other questions he needed answered.

"Did Bobby's aunt know about her nephew's little sideline?"

The guy turned his head to look at Cliff. "I dunno. Bobby sure didn't have much good to say about the ol' witch."

From down the road came another scream. "Cliff! I can't stop him! Help!" The out-of-control mule came racing back toward the cabin with his helpless rider on board.

"Damn!" Cliff leaped to his feet and ran to cut off the mule's flight. Tasha hadn't been playacting. The damn mule was a runaway.

"Daddy, the bad man's getting away!"

With a quick glance, Cliff saw the rustler had already made it into the woods on the other side of the road, lumbering through the trees, all but lost in the shadows. At the moment, Cliff was more worried about Tasha. He jockeyed into position and snared Henry's bridle. "Whoa! Henry. Damn it, whoa!"

With a final scream, Tasha slid off the saddle, arms flailing. She landed on the dirt with a grunt.

"Mommy!"

Catching the reins, Cliff dragged the mule away from Tasha so she wouldn't be trampled, and tied the animal to a tree. By the time he got to Tasha's side, both children were there and Tasha's eyes were wide-open, her jaw set at a grim angle.

"Give me your gun, Cliff," she breathlessly ordered, struggling to a sitting position. With her hand, she shoved back lank hair that had fallen across her face. Rain had begun to streak her cheeks with mud.

"The rustler's long gone, honey. We'll never catch—"

"I'm going to kill that mule, Clifford! I swear to—"

Cliff laughed out loud. He couldn't help himself. She looked so damn beautiful and he was so relieved they were all safe. Then he drew both the children and Tasha into his arms for the biggest hug he could muster.

Chapter Thirteen

"But I want to go home," Melissa complained. "Back to Uncle Cliff's house. Not New York."

Tasha pulled her daughter onto her lap, rocking her gently in the old wooden chair. They'd all shared a dozen hugs outside, a few admonishments for scaring Tasha and Cliff nearly to death and then they'd come inside the cabin to get out of the rain. Tasha hadn't gotten her revenge on Henry yet. Which was just as well. Her daughter was already too traumatized by being locked in this cabin with the rustler.

Through the grace of God, no other harm had come to the children except a good fright. It almost made Tasha forgive Henry his bizarre behavior—but not quite.

From what the children had told them, the rest of the rustlers wouldn't return for three or four days. And while the cabin wasn't spacious, it was comfortable with a living-eating area and a separate bedroom with bunk beds. Off the kitchen there was a bathroom of sorts, though without the luxury of hot-and-cold running water. What water they needed would come icy cold from a hand pump by the kitchen sink.

After getting them into the cabin, Cliff had gone back out to retrieve Sunny Boy from up the hill and to put all the animals in the corral behind the cabin.

"Honey, it would take us hours to get back to Cliff's," she told Melissa. "You've already been soaked through to the skin once and I'm afraid you'll catch a chill. Cliff says we should stay here the night and he's right."

"I stayed here with Ricky one time," Stevie said. "And I 'membered how to get here."

Tasha hooked an arm around the boy's shoulder. "It would have been better if you hadn't run off at all, Stevie. You could have gotten lost, or that bad man might have hurt you both."

He hung his head. "I didn't want Melissa to go."

"I know, son." Tasha blinked at the tears that filled her eyes. She was so terribly grateful the children were safe. Not that it changed what she had to do, but at least her plans to leave hadn't caused the children to come to serious harm.

But no way was she willing to ride that damn mule another hundred feet. She'd walk all the way to Reilly's Gulch before she did that.

"The bad man could come back," Melissa persisted.

"Cliff doesn't think so, honey. We're better off here for the night." The rain was coming down hard now, pounding on the cabin's tin roof like a snare drum. The potbellied stove in one corner of the room gave off a pleasant wave of heat along with the scent of burning wood. "Maybe by morning Uncle Bryant will find us."

A cell phone would have been nice to notify the authorities where they were and that Bobby Bruhn was the leader of the rustling ring. But this area was so remote and surrounded by hills, no communication was possible with the outside world without phone lines.

Both children brightened at the prospect of Bryant's rescuing them just as Cliff returned to the cabin. He dropped a load of bedrolls and saddlebags to the floor. Removing his hat, he slapped it against his thigh, spattering raindrops onto the pile.

"Horses are all put up for the night," he said. "Everything okay here?"

"We're fine," Tasha said. Not for the first time it struck her that Cliff was among the most competent men she'd ever known. There was almost nothing he couldn't do, from roping and riding to catching criminals. In contrast, she had little to offer such a man. The reality of their differences lodged in Tasha's throat as if she'd swallowed a stone.

"Let's see what we can find to eat." He shrugged out of his sheepskin jacket and hung it on the peg next to his hat.

Tasha eased Melissa off her lap. "I checked the cupboards. There're a couple of cans of chili con carne. I could heat them up."

"Great. If there's flour, we can have biscuits, too."

Biscuits? Clearly Cliff hadn't figured it out yet. Tasha was no Martha Stewart in the kitchen, certainly not with a wood-burning stove. "Have you got a recipe for biscuits?"

Cliff looked at her blankly.

"Aunt Ella makes us biscuits sometimes," Stevie said. "They're real fluffy."

"On Sunday mornings, my mommy buys us bagels from the bakery," Melissa said proudly.

Tasha looked at Cliff, mentally ticking off yet another of her inadequacies. "Just tell me what to do and I'll make the damn biscuits." She tried to stand, but every muscle in her body protested the slightest movement. She groaned.

"You stay put, sweetheart." Cliff rested his hand on her shoulder, applying gentle pressure that was little more than a caress. "You've had a long day. The kids and I will do dinner. Won't we, kids?"

The children cheered.

Tasha simply didn't have the energy to argue. Leaning back in the rocking chair, she watched the dinner preparations. With little effort, Cliff had the children bringing in kindling from the porch for the stove and setting out the mismatched silverware on the scarred dining table. He could have had an army of kids and they'd all perform beautifully. Meanwhile, he whipped up a batch of biscuits from scratch and popped them in the oven.

The man was a marvel!

Within a half hour, he had dinner on the table. The children ate hungrily, but Tasha could see they were almost as weary as she was. As soon as they'd finished their meal, she insisted the children pick out a bunk bed for themselves in the other room and get ready for bed.

As nearly as she could tell, both of them were asleep before their heads hit their pillows.

Giving them each a kiss, she returned to the living room to find Cliff still standing in the kitchen area. ''I'd give my right arm for a good soak in a hot tub about now,'' she said.

Cliff grinned at her and winked. ''Your every wish is my command, Ms. Goldilocks. I've already got the water heating.''

''You must be a mind reader.'' She'd seen the claw foot tub in the bathroom, but hadn't relished the idea of an icy cold bath. Now she quickly reconsidered her objection. That mule had left more than sore muscles on her person and she smelled terrible.

''I could use a bath, too, so don't expect to hog all the hot water.''

''I wouldn't think of it.''

''In fact...'' He walked to the door, made sure it was secured from the inside, then sauntered toward her. His blue eyes sparkled with mischief and masculine awareness. ''In order to economize, I figure we ought to share the tub.''

She swallowed hard and a slow curl of desire spun through her midsection. Moments ago she'd been bone weary; now all her fatigue had disappeared and she felt energized. ''At the same time?''

''I wouldn't want the water to cool off before I got my turn.'' He toyed with the top button of her blouse until it slipped loose from the hole.

''No. That wouldn't be fair.'' It also wasn't fair how much she'd miss Cliff after she returned to New York. Would it be worse...or better to have one more memory to carry with her? ''I wouldn't want the children to—'' The second button came free.

''I figure the kids are good for the night. They looked really beat at dinner.'' Another button and her shirt gaped open almost to her waist. He slid his hand inside, cupping her breast.

She drew a quick breath. ''Yes.'' It was almost a sigh. Certainly it was the husky sound of surrender. ''They were both asleep before I left the room.''

''Great.''

Without relinquishing his sensual hold on her breast, his mouth claimed hers in an equally erotic kiss. Her knees grew weak. This time the deficiency had nothing to do with riding a mule all day and everything to do with the man who was kissing her. Slowly and remorselessly.

''Cliff...''

''I know....''

He led her into the makeshift bathroom with its old-fashioned fixtures and plank floor covered only with a small oval hooked rug. She stood on the worn rug stripping her clothes off in the dim light cast by the kerosene lamp in the living room while he brought in pails of water, splashing them into the tub.

Time seemed to stand still. They'd entered another world, alien and distant from the reality Tasha had always known. A perfect world where her failures and limitations didn't matter.

When she looked into his eyes, she saw herself reflected there. A woman who was whole and desirable. She saw her softness, her weaknesses, as a counterpoint to his strength and enduring qualities.

As he stepped into the tub, drawing her after him, she let go of her insecurities. She could give herself to this man. For tonight she could be all that he wanted, all that he needed in this separate world they had found together. She'd be his golden sunrise. A vibrant field of purple lupine. The deep green of a forest or the verdant color of spring grass waving across the rolling countryside in a quickening breeze. A woman strong enough to match her man.

Joined together as one, they lathered each other, caressing, stroking, cleansing their spirits, giving and taking in this special time and place. Celebrating life. Exalting love.

And when their bodies finally demanded rest, Cliff dried Tasha with towels he found in a cupboard, her skin sensitized to the rough fabric where his callused hands had caressed her first. Then he wrapped them both in an old blanket and they slept on the lumpy couch in the living room, entwined together like loops of a hooked rug, forever linked together.

Sometime during the night, Tasha woke to the feel of tears on her cheeks. Their special world had vanished into the dark recesses of reality.

AT DAWN the next morning, Cliff was outside checking the horses when he heard the distinctive *thupp, thupp, thupp* of helicopter rotors in the distance. He hadn't wanted the kids to catch him and Tasha on the couch together, so he'd slipped out of their blanket cocoon early—at no small price to his libido, which had had other ideas.

Keeping an eye on the cloudless sky, he hurried back to the cabin to wake everyone. He opened the door and ducked his head inside.

The kids were up, Tasha was dressed and making an effort to comb Melissa's hair back into some semblance of a ponytail.

"Helicopter's coming," he told them.

The kids' eyes widened with excitement. Like a pair of eager puppies, they bolted away from Tasha and out the door, screaming and yelling. Cliff had to move fast to avoid being run over. Laughing, he stood in the doorway watching them wave to a still-empty sky.

"The pilot won't have to see those two to know we're here." Tasha joined him at the door. "I suspect everyone in Reilly's Gulch can hear them."

He slid her an admiring look, noting the healthy glow of her cheeks and the way she'd twisted her hair in a knot at her nape that was both casual and sophisticated. His heart filled with so much love, he thought it might burst.

"Have I told you that you were terrific yesterday luring the rustler out of the cabin?" he asked. Unable to resist, he fingered a loose strand of her hair, hooking it back over the delicate shell of her ear where it belonged.

"Terrific? I almost got myself killed on that fool mule."

"But you didn't and your plan worked."

She walked to the edge of the porch and hugged herself as she looked up at the sky watching for the helicopter to appear over the tops of the trees. "I don't belong here, Cliff."

His gut clenched. Whatever they'd shared last night meant nothing this morning. She was still going to leave him. "Just because you can't ride a mule? I should have gotten rid of Henry years ago."

"That's one reason," she said softly.

"And another one is that you don't want to give up your career."

She dipped her head, refusing to look at him.

Damn! He was helpless to argue with that and his pride wouldn't let him try. Every card-playing cowboy knew when to raise...and when to fold. Now was the time to fold.

He marched across the porch and down the steps to where the children were still screaming their heads off, even more excited now that the helicopter had appeared above the trees.

"Back on the porch, kids. Get out of the way so the 'copter can land."

"We're being rescued, Daddy."

"Yep, that's what it looks like." As the helicopter hovered, he saw that Bryant was riding shotgun with the state police pilot. He waved and his brother responded. "Come on, kids. Up on the porch." He herded them to safety. Moments later the helicopter landed in a blizzard of dust and pine needles.

Bryant was out of the cockpit before the rotors came to a full stop. Ducking, he ran toward the porch.

"Everybody okay?" he called.

"Everyone's fine," Tasha responded.

Cliff might have agreed with her except he felt an incredible weight filling his chest, no doubt a harbinger of things to come after she was gone.

The kids flew into Bryant's open arms. He hugged them both, then lifted Stevie. "Hey, young man, you know you just about scared Aunt Ella and me to death."

"I didn't mean to," the boy said solemnly. "But my daddy caught the bad guy who wouldn't let us go."

Thumbing his hat farther back on his head, Bryant shot his brother a questioning look. "What bad guy?"

Cliff brought him up to date, including the news that Bobby Bruhn was behind the rustling activity in the area. "If the Monroes had ever run a phone line out here, I would have called yesterday to let the sheriff know." Cliff shrugged. "No such luck."

"I'll be damned," Bryant said. "Not bad, you discovering who the rustlers are the day before the election and having the criminal turn out to be your opponent. I'd say if the election had ever been in doubt, it won't be once the word spreads about Bobby."

"Cliff will win for sure now, won't he?" Tasha asked, suddenly animated. Her eyes glistened.

"By a landslide. It'd be damn hard to explain ourselves if we elected a crook to office."

"I still have to prove the accusation," Cliff pointed out. "Right now I only have the word of a coconspirator, who's probably long gone from the county."

"You'll do it." Bryant extended his hand, his grin as wide as if he'd been elected, too. "Congratulations, Sheriff Swain. I'm proud of you, little Bro."

Cheering, Stevie dived for Cliff's arms and Tasha added her congratulations while Melissa gave him a hug around his midsection. He tried to feel excited about what he'd accomplished, an orphaned kid who'd worked his way up to being county sheriff. But his heart simply wasn't in it.

The thought of being sheriff without Tasha and her daughter as a part of his life made the victory a hollow one.

IT TOOK THEM a while to sort things out at the cabin but eventually they decided Tasha and the children would go back to town on board the helicopter. Understandably, Tasha was reluctant to ride any four-legged creature she had to straddle.

Meanwhile, Bryant and Cliff would take all the horses—and Henry—back to the ranch. With luck they'd arrive home by dinnertime. By then, the state police would notify Sheriff Colman to pick up Bobby Bruhn and his cohorts for questioning.

Squinting, Cliff watched the helicopter take off in another cloud of dust, then he turned toward the corral to saddle Sunny Boy. His legs felt as if they were filled with lead; his heart had turned to stone. If a bank robber had stepped right in his path and surrendered, Cliff wouldn't have given a damn. Some sheriff he made! He ought to resign, that was what he ought to do. He'd go back to punching cattle on the Double S. What the hell did it matter?

They'd been on the trail for an hour when Bryant spoke up. "It's going to be a helluva long ride if you're not going to talk at all."

Cliff glanced at his brother. "What's to say?"

"Maybe something about why you're so glum."

"I'm not glum. I'm great. I just assured my election to county sheriff, didn't I? Why shouldn't I be happy as a gopher in a carrot patch?"

"You tell me."

Cliff blew out a sigh. He couldn't keep much from his twin. There wasn't much point anyway since it was obvious Cliff felt as if he were on his way to a funeral instead of a campaign celebration. Not even the clear air after the storm or the budding wildflowers could raise his spirits. His thoughts had already slipped to New York where Tasha would soon be—a place he couldn't follow, not if he was to remain true to himself.

"You've got it really bad, haven't you?" Bryant asked.

Cliff nodded.

"Have you told her?"

"Told her what?"

"That you love her."

Cliff shifted uneasily in the saddle. Both he and Bryant had a couple of horses stringing along behind them, those that the kids had ridden in their great runaway escapade and those belonging to the rustlers. Plus Henry, of course. "It wouldn't make any difference. She's going back to the career she wants. Who am I to tell her different?"

"Maybe you're the man she loves and she's waiting for you to speak up first."

"Yeah, right. She loves me so much, she's getting in her car as soon as she can and heading for points east."

Bryant brought his horse up close beside Cliff's. "I almost lost Ella because I was too stupid to recognize what a good thing I'd found in her. I wouldn't want you to be as big a fool as I almost was."

Cliff was silent for a while as the horses plodded along. He was comfortable in the saddle but not with himself. "What'd you do?"

"Sal pointed out the only way I'd win Ella was to grovel. On my knees, if I had to."

In spite of himself, Cliff's lips twitched. "You? Grovel?"

"Damn right. I'd do it all over again, too." Bryant grinned. "In a heartbeat."

"I don't know." Tipping his hat back, Cliff looked off into the distance—into the past. "With Yvonne it was easy. We knew from seventh grade that we'd get married someday."

"Yeah, well, I found out the hard way these New York women are a little harder to corral than most."

Cliff pondered his brother's words for a minute.

"What if I...grovel...and she still goes back to New York?"

"You're at the end of your rope, Bro. Looks to me like you don't have anything to lose."

His brother had a good point. A little groveling never hurt anyone, assuming it was about something important. Tasha was. And so was the family Cliff wanted to create.

"I'll think about it," he said. Instinctively, he leaned forward so Sunny Boy would pick up the pace. It was a long way back home. And maybe, just maybe, he had one last chance to convince the woman he loved that Montana was exactly the place that offered all her heart desired.

Chapter Fourteen

It was almost dinnertime when Tasha heard a car arrive at the front of Cliff's house, and for an instant her heart leaped when she thought he must be back home. But then she realized he'd be returning with the horses, not driving.

She peered out the window and frowned.

It wasn't Cliff, but a red Mazda Miata convertible with an O'Reilly's Taxi Service placard stuck in the windshield.

She met Chester O'Reilly at the front door.

"Good afternoon, my dear." He swept off his red beret, bowing slightly. "I understand you and your family have had quite an adventure."

She smiled and held open the screen door for him. "A little more adventure than I'd bargained for," she conceded. "Please come in."

"Thank you. I won't take much of your time." Looking quite dapper, he was dressed in a Western-cut sport jacket and slacks and wore a silver-and-turquoise bolo tie.

She led him into the living room wondering what

had brought Chester to Cliff's house. The children were playing a noisy game of "helicopter pilots" out back, still excited about their ride home, and the sound of their make-believe motors was reassuring.

Gesturing for Chester to take the comfortable seat in front of the fireplace, she said, "What can I do for you?"

He declined the chair and remained standing, his hands clasped behind his back. "I am, my dear, an emissary here to ask not what you can do for me personally, but rather what we'd like you to do for the entire community of Reilly's Gulch."

"I don't understand." She really hoped he wasn't going to ask her to put on another fashion show. In the past few weeks she'd about used up all of the favors owed her and consumed every bit of organizational talent she possessed.

"As you might imagine, the news has spread rather quickly that Bobby Bruhn was behind all the recent cattle rustling activity in the neighborhood."

"Has Sheriff Colman arrested him?"

"He has. Apparently the young man tried to hide out at his Aunt Winifred's house. In the attic, I believe. She was quite appalled by his behavior. Cowardly, she says."

"She wasn't a part of it?"

"No, not at all. Winifred may often be vexatious to the spirit, and something of a busybody—"

Tasha could attest to that.

"—but she is at heart an honest woman with a great deal of respect for freedom of the press. She was frankly furious with her nephew that he had attempted to involve her and her newspaper in his nefarious schemes, a newspaper that her grandfather founded. She intends to publish a special edition of the *Register* tomorrow, throwing her support to Clifford. An admirable gesture, but a little too late.''

It would be nice if Winifred would also redeem Cliff's personal reputation and her own, Tasha thought, though after she left for New York hers wouldn't matter very much.

''In further penance for being taken in by her nephew's misdeeds,'' Chester continued, ''she submitted her resignation to the school board this afternoon at an emergency session.''

''That seems pretty sudden.'' Though it did raise Tasha's respect for the woman by one small notch. Still, snooping through people's windows...

''The remaining members of the school board have decided—informally, of course—that they wish to appoint Winnie's replacement to complete her term of office rather than hold another election so soon.''

''That seems reasonable.'' Even if Tasha didn't quite know where Chester was heading with this conversation. Perhaps they were thinking Cliff would make a good candidate. Although he couldn't serve on the school board and as sheriff.

''The person they would most like to see fill the vacant position is you.''

Having trouble processing his words, Tasha stared at the older gentleman, dumbfounded. ''Surely you mean Cliff—''

''Not at all. Though we are pleased he's to be our

new sheriff. We think you would bring to the school board new ideas and innovations, like the fashion show you so successfully organized.''

''The whole town has been gossiping about me and Cliff. Surely Preacher Goodfellow isn't about to support—''

''I believe he has been reconsidering his position since Winnie's resignation.''

''But I've never been anything more than a fashion model. I didn't even particularly like school when I was younger and my grades weren't all that swift. Naturally I'm flattered you'd want me, but I hardly think I'm the ideal candidate for the job. Surely there's someone else—''

''You're young and intelligent, the sort of person who's always been the backbone of Montana. I do wish you'd accept the school board's offer.''

She sat down heavily on the padded arm of the couch. No one had ever thought of her as intelligent. People rarely looked past her physical features. If anything, what they saw was a dumb blonde. And now the school board was asking *her* to join them in a leadership role? It hardly seemed possible.

In fact, it was impossible.

''Chester, I'm not planning to stay in Montana.''

''Oh, dear.'' He sat down on the edge of the coffee table in front of her. ''I hadn't expected that complication. We assumed…that is, after these past few weeks, we thought you and Clifford—''

''No.'' She tugged her lower lip between her teeth. ''I'll be leaving for New York in the next day or so. I have a big job lined up. I get to be a spokesperson for—'' Her voice cracked and tears flooded her eyes. ''It's a wonderful opportunity.''

''And you're crying because it's so wonderful.''

She nodded.

Sympathy filled his gray eyes. ''You are much like my dear departed wife. Penelope always cried when she was happy.''

''Sometimes women do that.'' She tried to swallow her tears without complete success. One spilled down her cheek.

Chester's hand covered Tasha's, his fingers twisted by arthritis. ''Penelope also cried when I upset her. Has Clifford upset you, my dear?''

''It's not his fault. It's just that I—I can't stay. I can't be the wife he needs.''

''That makes me doubly sad.'' He gave her hand a gentle pat. ''You see, I had hoped if you were to stay, you'd decide you needed a pickup or a sport utility vehicle to replace your BMW. It's a Montana thing to do. And my taxi business is flourishing. Your car would make a nice addition to my fleet.''

Despite the ache in her heart, Tasha smiled. ''I'm sorry.''

''Yes, well...'' Standing, he carefully placed his cap on his head at a jaunty angle. ''I must say, until now I thought Clifford to be a bright young man with a grand future. But if he is letting you go...'' Chester shook his head. ''If I were a younger man, I'd certainly do everything in my power to get you to stay.''

She stood and kissed him on his leathery cheek.

"You're sweet, Chester. If you were a bit younger, I just might do it, too."

With another bow, he left. Tasha stood on the front porch watching him drive his Mazda ever so slowly down the drive and turn onto the street right in front of an oncoming car. Brakes squealed, but Chester seemed unaware of the disaster he'd barely averted.

Hugging herself, Tasha found it amazing that she'd had to travel all the way to Montana to have someone recognize there was more to her than physical beauty. She'd never expected Reilly's Gulch to accept her as anything but an outsider. Yet now they'd asked her to be on their school board—an invitation she couldn't accept.

She'd never be able to remain in Reilly's Gulch without being Cliff's wife. It would be too painful to see him and not be able to love him. And she couldn't marry Cliff, even if he asked her, because she couldn't give him the children he wanted. So she was right back where she started—packing her bags.

Her chin trembled and she turned away from the view of the empty road she'd take tomorrow on her way to New York.

The phone rang as she stepped inside. It was Sylvia, Cliff's housekeeper, calling to say she was back in town and ready to start work again. With a deep sense of regret burning in her stomach, Tasha told the woman her timing was perfect.

"AND THE 'copter swooped *way* up in the sky." Stevie demonstrated, his hand skimming over his dinner plate and climbing fast to miss the carton of milk on the table. "An' it was real noisy. We could hardly even talk to each other."

"We saw a whole bunch of moose," Melissa added. "They looked like little ants running through the trees."

"Pretty exciting ride, huh?" Cliff smiled at the youngsters, who had pretty much devoured the hamburgers Tasha had made for dinner. In contrast, Cliff didn't have much of an appetite. He mentally ticked off the minutes until the kids would be in bed and it would be his turn to grovel. Every swallow came hard. *God, what if she turned him down?*

"Can we do it again, Daddy? Can we, huh? Please."

"I don't know, son. Those helicopters are used only for official business."

"You're the sheriff so you're 'ffical, aren't you?"

"Not quite, not till after the election tomorrow. But that's not how it works anyway." Frowning at his son's leap of logic, he glanced toward Tasha, who was sitting opposite him, the food on her plate barely touched. An amused smile played at the corners of her lips, but there was a hint of sadness in the deep blue of her eyes. In his gut, Cliff hoped it was because she was as reluctant to leave as he was to have her go.

Her gaze held his for a moment, then slid away. "Children, if you're done with your dinner, you can go get washed up for bed."

"But we wanna play 'copter pilots some more," Stevie complained.

"Melissa and I have to get up early tomorrow," Tasha said quietly.

Stevie hung his head; so did Melissa. Cliff had the urge to follow suit, but he'd never been a quitter. He wasn't going to start now.

He shoved back from the table. "Look, kids, you go get cleaned up and ready for bed. I'm going to take Tasha for a walk outside and maybe when we come back we'll have a surprise—"

Her head came up, her eyes questioning him.

"Well, we'll talk about that later."

He shooed the youngsters out of the kitchen. Leaving the dirty dishes on the table, he took Tasha's arm and escorted her out the back door. The stars were just appearing in the sky. To the west, the last of the sunset had turned the clouds above the Rockies a pale pink.

"What's going on, Cliff?"

"I've got something to say…something to ask you, actually, and I didn't want an audience."

"I see."

He wasn't sure what the best venue for groveling might be. He didn't want to take her out by the corral where she'd remember she hated horses—and mules. So he walked her around to the front of the house, up on the porch and sat her down in the old swing. The chains creaked when he sat down beside her.

He cleared his throat. "I know you're excited about being a spokesperson for the shampoo company. And New York's real metropolitan and has stuff like ballet and the theater that we don't have here in Reilly's Gulch. Hell, we don't even have a movie theater.''

''I haven't missed those things as much as I thought I would.''

He took that as an encouraging sign. ''I want you to know I think you're the most wonderful, most beautiful and intelligent woman I've ever known. And Melissa's great, too.''

''Thank you.''

''You're welcome.'' This wasn't going as he had hoped. For hours he'd practiced this damn speech and it wasn't coming out right.

''What are you trying to say?''

''That I…that I love you and want you to marry me,'' he finally blurted out all in one breath. ''Say yes, Tasha. Please.''

''I can't, Cliff.''

''Look, you can visit New York anytime you want. You can even do the commercials, if they're important to you. I just want you to come back to me. I want this to be your home. I want us, the four of us, to be a family.''

Her eyes glistening with tears, she palmed his face, her hand cool and feminine against his cheek. Cliff had the terrible feeling he'd lost. He'd groveled as best he could and still she didn't want to be his wife.

''Have you forgotten what I told you? Why I can't be the wife you deserve?''

He blinked. He didn't remember her telling him anything like that. "What are you talking about?"

"Your plans for this house, all those bedrooms you wanted to add on upstairs..." Her voice faltered, her hand dropped to her lap. "I'm so sorry I can't fill them for you."

Slowly, like the forks of a meandering stream coming back together, things fell into place for him. What she'd told him about was not being able to have babies. Even why she'd been engaged to a man she didn't love—because she thought she wasn't good enough for someone else.

"Goldilocks, look at me."

She raised her head. In the last light from the sun he could see tear tracks on her cheeks.

"Do you love me?" he asked and held his breath.

"So much that I want you to have that big family you've always wanted. And I can't—"

"Listen to me." He bent forward, silencing her by kissing her tears away. "The only bedroom I'm worried about filling is my own. With *you.* I've got Stevie and you've got Melissa. I'd say that was a pretty darn perfect family, just the four of us. What I feel for you is too special to throw away just because we can't have more kids. I don't want to make that big a sacrifice. I don't want you to, either."

Tasha tried to speak, but so much emotion filled her chest she could barely breath. "Are you sure I'd be enough for you?"

"So sure—" he pulled her into his arms and held her close "—in fact, if the only way I can have you is to give up my job as sheriff and move to New

York or L.A. so you can have the career you want, I'll do it. I swear, I will.''

His words filled her with such joy, she could barely contain it…along with a quick burst of anger. She planted her palms on his chest and shoved him away.

"Clifford Swain, I busted my butt helping to get you elected! There's no way I'm going to let you give that up, do you hear me? Tomorrow they'll declare you the winner and you'll be the best sheriff this county has ever seen.''

He looked a little stunned. "I just thought—"

"Are you saying I wouldn't make a good enough sheriff's wife because I can't iron your shirts worth beans?''

"I'm gonna switch to no-iron uniforms.''

"I should hope so. And how 'bout my cooking? If I agree to be your wife, I certainly hope you don't plan to fire Sylvia and make me work for free. I've got better things to do with my time besides making fancy casseroles.''

"You do?''

"I've been thinking about selling my car, too. One of the sturdy SUVs makes a lot more sense for a Montana housewife with a couple of kids to haul around than a sedan.''

"You think so?''

"Yep.'' Her happiness—including her relief that she hadn't signed a contract—finally burst free into a smile so wide it almost hurt. "I've made a decent living being a model, but I've always dreamed of being something more than a pretty face and good figure. Someone who was respected for what she could *do,* not just what she looked like. With you, and the people of Reilly's Gulch, I've found that self-respect I've been searching for. I'll never miss doing the shampoo commercial. Not for a minute.''

His lips twitched into a smile almost as broad as hers. ''You're sure?''

''Absolutely. Besides, I'm going to take Winifred's place on the school board. Chester came by to ask me this afternoon. Given the problems around here, I expect that job—which doesn't pay a dime, by the way—will keep me busy.''

''I suppose it would.''

''But not so busy it would keep me out of your bed,'' she said slyly.

''I'm really glad to hear that.'' He reached for her again, catching the back of her head as he drew her closer. ''How 'bout we seal this bargain with a kiss?''

''I thought you'd never ask.''

Eagerly her mouth sought his, seeking his warmth and the sweet caress of his tongue. As he kissed her, Tasha felt whole. This time it was no illusion, no dreamworld made from her fantasies, but something real and enduring. He loved her as she was, flaws and limitations included. And she loved him.

Vaguely, as the kiss continued, she was aware of the screen door on the porch opening.

''My mommy's kissing your daddy,'' came a young voice in a stage whisper.

''Oh, yuck. How come they're doing that?''

"I'm not sure, but I think it means I'm going to get to stay here forever 'n ever."

"Well, then, I guess it's okay. Let's go see if there's ice cream in the freezer. I bet that's the surprise Daddy wanted to tell us about."

The door hinge creaked again and the latch caught.

Tasha smiled to herself. Life was full of surprises. Coming to Montana and falling in love with Cliff, having him love her in return, was the nicest one she'd ever had.

She leaned back and looked into Cliff's dark eyes and sensed the passion he felt. "We're going to have a wonderful life, aren't we?"

"Absolutely, Goldilocks. I promise you'll find it's *just right* for all four of us."

Look for an exciting new trilogy from Charlotte Maclay, on sale 2001 in Harlequin American Romance.

If you enjoyed what you just read,
then we've got an offer you can't resist!

Take 2 bestselling love stories FREE!

Plus get a FREE surprise gift!

A special feeling,
  A special secret...
    No one blossoms more beautifully
      than a woman who's

With Child...

And the right man for her
will cherish the gift of love she brings.

**Join American Romance and four
wonderful authors for the event of a lifetime!**

THAT'S *OUR* BABY!
Pamela Browning
March 2000

HAVING THE BILLIONAIRE'S BABY
Ann Haven
April 2000

THAT NIGHT WE MADE BABY
Mary Anne Wilson
May 2000

MY LITTLE ONE
Linda Randall Wisdom
June 2000

Available at your favorite retail outlet.

HARLEQUIN®
Makes any time special ™

Visit us at www.romance.net

HARWC

Coming in June from

When two sets
of twins are born at
Maitland Maternity Hospital on
the same day, unforgettable surprises
are sure to follow. Don't miss the fun, the
romance, the joy...as two special couples find
love just outside the delivery room door.

Watch for:
SURPRISE! SURPRISE!
by Tina Leonard
On sale June 2000.

I DO! I DO!
by Jacqueline Diamond
On sale July 2000.

And there will be many more Maitland Maternity
stories when a special twelve-book continuity series
launches in August 2000.
Don't miss any of these stories by wonderful
authors such as Marie Ferrarella, Jule McBride,
Muriel Jensen and Judy Christenberry.

Available at your favorite retail outlet.

Visit us at www.eHarlequin.com.

HARMMDD

COMING NEXT MONTH

#829 SURPRISE! SURPRISE! by Tina Leonard
Maitland Maternity: Double Deliveries
After months of trying to conceive, Maddie Winston had finally become the proud mother of twins. But how could she tell her husband, Sam, that she'd raided his sperm bank "deposit" during their yearlong separation? Would two bundles of joy be enough to teach Maddie and Sam that love could overcome all obstacles?

#830 THE RANCHER'S MAIL-ORDER BRIDE by Mindy Neff
Bachelors of Shotgun Ridge
The grizzled matchmakers of Shotgun Ridge, Montana, had found Wyatt Malone the perfect mail-order bride...without letting the solitary rancher know. Though Wyatt may not have volunteered for the position, he was gonna be the first man to help repopulate their little town—whether he liked it or not!

#831 MY LITTLE ONE by Linda Randall Wisdom
With Child...
Her supposedly innocent blind date had turned into one night to remember! Though her charming escort, Brian Walker, had saved her from serious injury and satiated her every need, Gail was certain she'd never see him again. Until she discovered a little one was on the way....

#832 DOCTOR, DARLING by Jo Leigh
When he unknowingly broke a one-hundred-and-twenty-five-year-old law, Dr. Connor Malloy was sentenced to take Gillian Bates on a date. But Gillian was hardly the spinster he expected. How long would it be before the intelligent beauty had Connor realizing that one night with Gillian wasn't going to be nearly enough?

Visit us at www.eHarlequin.com